Such Redemption as This

Rebecca Velez

Cheryl,

"The Lord redeems the
soul of his servants,
and none of those who
take refuge in Him will
be condemned."

Your friend,

Becky Velez

Such Redemption as This

Published in the U.S. by Rebecca Velez Books
Manchester, NH

Cover by Carpe Librum Book Design

Scripture portions are taken from a combination of versions:
The Holy Bible, King James Version.
The New International Version®. NIV®. Copyright © 1973, 1978, 1984 by International Bible Society. Used by permission of Zondervan. All rights reserved.
The New American Standard Bible®, copyright © 1960, 1962, 1963, 1968, 1971, 1972, 1973, 1975, 1977, 1995 by The Lockman Foundation. Used by permission.

ISBN: 978-1-7322921-4-7
Library of Congress Control Number: 2018905639

Dedicated to Mothers and Daughters,
especially Alyssa

Such a Hope Series

Such a Time as This
Such Deliverance as This
Such Redemption as This

Redeem me, O Lord, the God
of truth
Psalm 31:5

Cast of Characters

(Historical figures in bold)

Abigail—Tobiah's Jewish wife
Ariel—Naama's husband
Artaxerxes—King of Persia 465-424 BC
Artystone—Naama's mother, a weaver of Persian rugs

Benjamin—husband of Hadassah, former husband of Judith

Ctesias—Judith's husband, Persian merchant

Dael—Benjamin's brother, merchant in Rabbah
David—Yael's betrothed

Eden—wife of Johanan
Eliashib—high priest in the Jerusalem temple
Enoch—David's uncle, Gibeonite
Esther—Persian queen
Ezra—priestly leader to Judah in 458 BC

Gili—Ariel's cousin

Hadassah—Ezra's eldest daughter, Benjamin's wife

Joiada—the high priest's eldest son
Jarah—Oren's wife
Johanan—Tobiah's eldest son
Judith—Ammonite wife of Ctesias, former wife of Benjamin

Leyla—Dael's Ammonite wife

Mary—Benjamin's youngest sister
Menachem—Tova's husband

Naama—proselytized Jew who returns to Judah, wife of Ariel
Nehemiah—king Artaxerxes' cupbearer, governor (Tirshatha) of Yehud
Noa—daughter of Tobiah and Abigail

Oren—leader in Gibeon, Jarah's husband

Rachel—Hadassah's daughter, named for her deceased grandmother

Samuel—Ezra's son-in-law, Gibeonite
Sparamizes—Esther's deceased, adopted son

Tova—Ammonite woman married to Menachem the Jew
Tobiah—Ammonite leader, Judith's brother, Abigail's husband

Jewish time

First watch   sunset to 9 p.m.
Second watch   9 p.m. to midnight
Third watch   midnight to 3 a.m.
Fourth watch   3 a.m. to sunrise

Glossary

Abba—Hebrew for father

Ahura-Mazda—Zoroastrian deity of good

Apadana—audience hall for the king and his subjects

Bet 'amma—house of the people, later called a synagogue

Em—Hebrew word for mother

Kohl—black eye make-up

Matok –Hebrew word for sweet one

Moloch—Ammonite god

Noruz—Persian New Year's festival

Parasang—Persian measure of distance, about 3 miles

Peshach—Passover

Shalom—literally peace, a greeting of hello or good-bye

Shekel—unit of currency based on a unit of weight, four days' pay

Softa—Hebrew word for grandmother

Span—9-10 inches

Tirshatha—governor

Yehud—the Persian satrapy (district) including Judah

House of Ezra

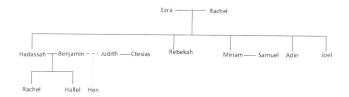

Family of Naama

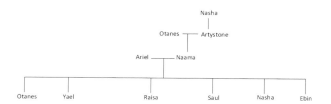

House of Oren

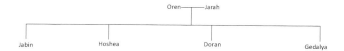

House of Tobiah

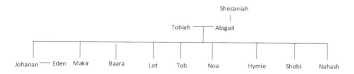

1

Naama paused from knotting the blue and tan rug to lift her face and soak up the sun. Fat buds burst from healthy grape vines as far as she could see.

Contentment seeped into her soul, and a smile lighted her face. She had loathed this place. Feared it would not support the family she desired, this scrap of land in *Yehud* that drew her husband Ariel from their home and family in Susa.

Her *em* told her returning to the Promised Land of the Jews would be a blessing. As always, her mother was right. Fourteen years later Naama could finally appreciate her wisdom.

Bees buzzed in springtime flowers. Yael had planted purple spears in a cracked pot and placed it in the courtyard of their limestone cottage. Their home had grown from one rude room to three spaces surrounding an open courtyard. Stout branches spanned the central area. Leafy vines provided shade in the summer, but allowed sunlight to warm the space during cooler months.

Toddler Ebin slept under a wool blanket in a sheltered corner. Naama's oldest daughters Yael and Raisa were fetching water from Gibeon's well. Seven-year-old Saul and five-year-old Nasha were playing in the vineyard but would return soon for dinner.

Neighing alerted Naama to strangers on the path winding through the vineyard. Yael and Raisa appeared first, eyes wide in pale faces. "There's a man here to see you, em," ten-year-old Raisa said.

Naama rose and brushed blue fibers from her robe. Laying one hand on each of her daughters, she greeted a finely dressed Ammonite with a small retinue of servants.

"It's a fine vineyard," he said. "Larger and healthier than the last time I was here."

Fingers of fear snatched at Naama as she struggled to remember him.

"It was before your time," he explained. "Could I have a drink?"

Responding to the note of command in his voice, Yael scurried inside for a cup, scooped water from her clay pot, and offered it to the mounted man. He drank and passed it to the younger man on his right. The two shared a family resemblance, but the teen looked kinder than his haughty father.

"I've come on a business matter."

"My husband's not home presently, sir. We expect him any time."

"I am Tobiah of Rabbah. I was conducting business in Jerusalem and decided to stop here in Gibeon to look after my sister's affairs. This vineyard was the dowry of my sister Judith when she married Benjamin son of Isaak. He divorced her but did not return the land nor its price."

Naama sank to a bench. *Where is Ariel? How would he answer this man?*

"I don't know anything about this. Judith only lived here for a short time when my family first arrived. Benjamin moved away about a year after." The poor man had up and left one winter's day, unable to deal with the memories of his wife and dead daughter.

"My sister owns this property. It's in this marriage contract." The man held up a clay tablet. "She has no

2

desire to turn you out of your home. She'd like payment of fifty *shekels*."

Naama gasped. Ariel kept five silver shekels in the house. He was in Jerusalem selling aged wine and purchasing supplies. He might return with fifteen more. "We...we don't have that much money. Could you camp for the night and speak with my husband and the elders tomorrow?" *Please, Lord, bring Ariel home.*

"I have business to attend. This matter has already consumed the best hours of the day."

"Could I pay part of the price now and the rest later?"

"It needs to be at least half."

Naama staggered into the house and shook their coins out of a carved box. Maybe there would be more than she thought. No, only three. *Ariel must have needed the other two for his trip. How much would he bring home? Surely not twenty-two shekels.* She frantically searched their quarters, looking for anything of value. Her rugs were valuable, but none were complete except an old rug her mother wove years ago. It wouldn't be worth much now.

She returned to find Tobiah eying Yael wolfishly. Swallowing hard, she held out a bag with the three coins. "This is all we have. My husband is selling wine and will bring more."

"How many jugs of wine did he have to sell?"

"Ten jugs of aged wine."

"They won't bring twenty-two shekels," he said harshly.

"No," she admitted, eyes downcast.

"I'll take the girl." He pointed to Yael. "How old are you?"

"Twelve," Yael squeaked.

"A young female servant is worth about fifteen shekels."

"She's betrothed, sir."

"Maybe the bridegroom's family will redeem her."

Naama turned to Raisa and whispered, "Run to David's house. Tell them what's happening. Ask for him and his kinsmen to come *immediately*. If you don't see Gili, ask someone to look for him and send him to the vineyard. Take the little ones with you, except for Ebin. I'll keep him here."

"I'm sure they'll be able to help," Naama announced to her unwanted visitors, trying to keep her voice steady. "I need to make bread. If you'd like to rest in the shade, they'll arrive soon." She picked up her slumbering son and retreated to her indoor hearth with Yael, away from prying eyes.

"Em?" Yael's brown eyes shone with fear. Naama wrapped an arm around her petite firstborn. "Em, are they going to take me away? David doesn't have any money. His father's been sick so long." Her shoulders began to shake as she cried silently.

"I know, child, but I pray he will bring his Uncle Enoch and he'll know what to do."

"They don't have money either..."

"Pray, Yael, and while you pray make some more barley meal." Naama handed her the mortar and pestle. "I'm going to use all you made yesterday."

"Are we making enough for the men outside?"

"Not on your life!"

The unleavened bread was browning on a stone when Raisa reappeared. "David, Enoch, and Samuel are outside with those awful men. I couldn't find Gili."

"Good job, Raisa. Where are the little ones?"

"David's Aunt Mary kept them with her."

"Praise be to Adonai! Raisa, you stay here and make sure the bread doesn't burn. When it's done, put another slab of dough on the stone. Feed Ebin if he gets cranky, but stay in here with your brother, no matter what."

"Yes, Em."

"Come, Yael." Naama took her trembling arm and squeezed it reassuringly. Yael's pleading eyes connected with hers.

4

As they walked silently into the space in front of the courtyard, they heard Enoch arguing, "You can't swoop into a Jewish village and take a daughter of Judah."

"This debt has been owed my family for thirteen years," Tobiah retorted.

"It was Judith's dowry. Where is she?" Enoch asked.

"I'm collecting it on her behalf."

"Why now, after all these years?" David asked.

"My father recently passed into the next life. I've been sorting through his business affairs and found this tablet."

"May I see it?" Samuel, the only literate one in their group, requested. Tobiah handed it to him. After reading it, Samuel admitted, "This is the marriage contract for Judith the Ammonite. Her dowry was this vineyard. The bride price was goats. It specifies the vineyard is Judith's in the event of divorce."

"My sister was divorced and cast out of this community. She has no desire to remain the owner of this vineyard or deal with tenants. She wants the cost of the vineyard. Fifty shekels is a fair price."

"It is a fair price," Enoch said, "But requiring it with no notice while the head of the family is gone is *not*."

"It's been thirteen years. We could ask for interest."

"I'll go!" The words burst out of Yael. *Maybe, somehow, David and her family could gather fifty shekels. They would never be able to pay thirteen years' interest too.*

Naama froze. "No, please. Wait for my husband to return."

"I have no more time for this matter," Tobiah said harshly. "You've paid me three shekels. These villagers brought five more. I'll take the girl as a slave for now. Redeem her after this year's harvest for fifteen shekels. You'll owe me twenty-seven more." He motioned to his men who mounted quickly.

The young man pulled Yael up behind him on his fine chestnut mare. Stunned, she sat like a sack of grain.

"Yael, hold onto him so you don't fall off," David said.

"Wait, she'll need another robe and a few things."
Spinning on her heel, Naama rushed into their sleeping
space and grabbed a robe and tunic, stuffing them into a
cracked goatskin bag.

When she reached her daughter, she clasped her hand
while pressing the bag into it. "Go with God, daughter."

Yael didn't have time to reply as the riders whirled
their mounts and trotted up the road.

2

Grabbing her horseman's robe didn't give Yael much stability.

"Hold onto my waist," he commanded.

Relieved to have her bag as a buffer, she stuffed it between them and grasped his waist. Embarrassed by touching a man so intimately, she mumbled, "I've never ridden a horse."

"I can tell. Try to move with the horse instead of bouncing down when she's coming up. We only have a few more hours of daylight before we'll stop to camp."

Even though she concentrated on the horse's movement, she never found its rhythm and almost fell when her legs buckled as she tried to dismount. Her rider, who had introduced himself as Johanan, steadied her before joining the others to set up camp.

Yael walked to ease the soreness. She cringed to think how she'd feel after a full day of riding. How many days would they ride? When would she return home? And what would tonight hold? She was encamped in the open with five men. Silent tears tracked down her face. *I'd better stay awake and alert until they're sleeping.*

But as soon as she choked down some bread and figs, Yael fell into an exhausted sleep on a goatskin Johanan offered her. Before dawn, he shook her awake, and they were riding before the morning star set. "If we ride hard today, we'll reach Rabbah tomorrow."

Adonai, I don't know how I'm going to stay on this horse until then. And how will my family redeem me and pay for the vineyard?

⌘⌘

Naama shrieked when she saw her husband leading the donkey up the vineyard path. She ran to tell him about the Ammonite and Yael, but when she reached him she could only sob. "Yael, Ariel...he took...our Yael."

"I know," Ariel said grimly. "David met me outside the gates and told me the whole sorry story." He embraced his wife. "Tobiah frequents Jerusalem. Oren said he married one of gatekeeper Shecaniah's daughters. He forces Shecaniah to do him favors by hinting he'll harm Abigail if Shecaniah doesn't comply. Disgusting pagan!"

"And now he has our daughter," Naama wailed. "It feels like they cut out my heart. She's such a good girl."

Naama sprang out of his arms. "David didn't break the betrothal, did he? She loves him with all her being, has loved him since she was a tiny girl."

"No, no. He's broken-hearted and desperate to get her back."

"Did you bring any coins? That heathen said she's worth fifteen shekels."

"I thought I did well. Twelve shekels from the wine, but I spent two on supplies."

"I gave him the three we had. And Enoch gave him five, so now we owe him too."

"We *will* redeem Yael at harvest," Ariel promised, "even if I have to borrow silver from Rabbi Ezra himself." He gazed at the vineyard he'd worked for fourteen back-breaking years. "But I don't know how we'll save the vineyard. It's worth double the price he named because of the improvements done since it was Judith's dowry, but we can't earn the sum he's demanding in six moons."

"My rug! It will fetch a good price at the market in Jerusalem."

"How close are you to finishing it?"

"If I work on it day and night, I'll be able to finish so you can take it with the wine we make at harvest. But who will do the washing and baking? Even with Yael and I both working, we labored all day. Raisa can do a little more, but..." Naama's voice trailed off sadly.

"We'll find a way. Jarah can do some of your tasks. She and Oren are settling in, but she said she'd come as soon as she could."

Naama cried again when she saw the bulk of her best friend on the dirt path cutting through the center of the vineyard. "Hush, now," Jarah comforted her with a hug.

"I'm so scared for Yael. What if they hurt her, steal her virginity? Harvest is a long way off, and that man has the morals of a tax collector."

"We will pray, and we'll work," Jarah promised. "I wish I hadn't bought the house in Jerusalem with my weaving money. It would have kept Yael safely here, even if it didn't cover the whole cost of the vineyard."

Naama leaned back from her friend. "I don't think so," she said slowly. "Tobiah had this cruel, predatory look. He wanted Yael. He would have demanded the whole sum at once. I don't understand why though. She's just a coltish girl, not even a woman, and certainly no great beauty."

"He's the kind of man who relishes causing pain. His business in Jerusalem is minimal, but he shows up every few moons to torment Shecaniah. I've seen Abigail a few times over her twenty-year marriage, and she looks well, not skinny or skittish from being mistreated. He may be like thunderclouds that bring no rain."

"I pray so. At least I know he has a Jewish wife to look out for Yael. I think if I can finish my rug, we'll have plenty to redeem her."

"I thought you just started it." Jarah regretted her words, seeing the look in her friend's eyes. Normally it took a year to finish a rug.

"I have almost a *span* completed. I'm going to have to work night and day on it."

"Then my boys and I will do all we can to fetch your water and work in the vineyard so you can weave. Let me collect your water pots. I'll have my boys take turns delivering your water. If you have Raisa grind your meal and bring it to me, I'll make leavened bread."

Naama smiled in relief. "That would be a huge help. Raisa can make the unleavened bread and our stews. Oren and David and Gili can handle the vineyard except at harvest when everyone pitches in."

"Do you have enough yarn to finish?"

"Yes, I always dye enough before I start so the colors are consistent."

After Jarah took their water pots back to town, Naama settled down to knot the fibers of her newest rug. She no longer admired the view or paused to soak in the spring warmth as on the previous day. Her fingers flew as she pleaded, *Adonai, defender of the weak and helpless, place a hedge of protection around my daughter.*

10

3

Judith dressed in violet silk with great care. Finally, she would dine at the winter palace in Susa. Her maid Sasha clasped a gold chain with a pearl pendant around her mistress' neck. Judith scrutinized herself in a bronze mirror. *What would the other women wear*?

Proudly she stood behind her husband Ctesias as they were admitted at the palace gate. She had visited the grounds when the roses were in bloom but King Artaxerxes and his queen were not in residence. At this time of year, the bushes were dormant. They passed to the right of the huge pool in front of the *apadana* to the state dining room.

Susa's elite were reclining on gold and silver couches around low tables. Judith greeted several of the leaders' wives with a kiss on the cheek as Ctesias guided them toward their allotted place in the middle of the great room. As one of the city's wealthiest merchant families, they were seated with other businessmen, including several families of jewelers. *My necklace is as fine as anything these women are wearing, but I'd like an emerald pendant like the jeweler's pudgy wife.*

"Enjoying yourself, my dear?" Ctesias whispered.

"Absolutely. I've been waiting to dine at one of the king's banquets since we arrived in Susa thirteen years ago."

"You've always been huge with child when the king announced one," Ctesias answered with satisfaction. "Three fine sons you've given me." He leaned closer. "We can try for another tonight."

Good. Her husband would share her bed tonight instead of sleeping with his other wife. She suspected she was already with child since she'd missed her monthly bleeding, but it was too soon to tell her husband. She smiled at him flirtatiously.

When he returned his attention to their fellow guests, Judith scanned the pillared room, searching for the most beautiful woman in attendance. The queen was best dressed, but her neck was scrawny and her face pale under the *kohl*. A striking Indian draped in a fuchsia sari caught her eye.

Eventually Judith settled on an olive-skinned figure seated in one of the lowliest spots, far from the king. *This woman's elegance might outshine me. Who is her husband?*

Judith sputtered and choked on her wine. Ctesias looked at her in alarm, but Judith shook her head to indicate she would recover.

The woman's husband was none other than her former husband Benjamin. *How can he be here? He's supposed to be dead.*

She glanced at Ctesias who had followed her gaze to the far corner of the room. His eyes fastened on the Jewish goddess. Judith fumed at the interest sparking in them, but was relieved he didn't recognize her former husband.

12

Why should he? They had never formally met. But she had asked for Benjamin's death when she first agreed to be Ctesias' wife and he said his men killed Benjamin. Did they kill the wrong man, or had he lied?

Musicians filled the space in front of the king, and all the guests turned their attention to the lute and harp players, blocking Judith's view of her first husband and his exquisite companion. By the time the performance ended, Benjamin and his wife had disappeared.

⌘⌘

As Hadassah followed Benjamin from the columned hall, she worried Esther would not survive the night. When her husband noticed her fidgeting, he announced they were returning to their vigil.

As they walked past the reflecting pool to Esther's tower rooms, Hadassah smiled gratefully at the husband who understood her well, remembering their inauspicious beginning.

⌘⌘

Eight years ago, Hadassah had answered a knock at the door of the temple chamber she shared with her father. "Hanani, it's so good to see you! Let me get you some water."

The king's courier had sunk exhausted onto a bench against the wall. "I apologize for my appearance, but this letter from the king is urgent."

Hadassah handed him a cup and accepted the parchment. "For my father?"

"No, my lady, not for Rabbi Ezra, but for you."

Hadassah's eyes widened and her face drained. "The Queen...Esther...is she...?"

"Alive when I left, but had lost the use of the right side of her body. Sit and read the letter. It will explain."

Hadassah sank to a small stool near the open door. Her brow furrowed as she scanned the king's missive. "He's asked me to return to care for her."

"I know. I'm your escort if you'll go."

"Of course I'll go. She's like a mother to me, but...what if we're too late?"

"Her times are in the Almighty's hands. We'll ride as fast as we can. I made the journey in two moons."

"Two moons! That's half the time it took us to travel here from Babylon five years ago."

"We won't be herding animals or caring for children." Hanani finished his wine and returned the cup.

"I've never ridden a horse." Hadassah fidgeted with the cup.

"Are you willing to learn? It's the fastest way to travel."

"Is it hard?"

"No, but I'd like to spend a few days getting you used to riding, before we leave."

"I'll give it a try, but I need my father's consent to return to Susa. He's serving in the temple. Come eat with us tonight, and I'll have an answer for you."

Her father had acquiesced, but he wanted her to marry first. His hasty arrangement of a second marriage stunned her, but she wanted to return to care for Esther, so she became Benjamin's wife.

14

Now Hadassah held the former queen's hand. The beautiful face that had won a kingdom was lined with pain. Her breathing was slow and raspy.

"It won't be long," the court physician said.

Hadassah nodded sadly.

"The king hasn't changed his mind?" he whispered.

"He hasn't wanted to see her since she became debilitated. It's too hard. He wants to remember her the way she was."

"It's a difficult thing to see." The doctor sighed. "You've provided excellent care. Not many patients recover as fully as she did from her first episode."

Hadassah stroked her hand. "The God of our fathers had mercy on her. She lived seven more years, although her health has been fading steadily this last year."

"She's only been incapacitated this last moon. She lived well until she fell down the steps." The doctor retreated to a chair under one of the windows of Esther's tower room.

"Yes, God is good." Hadassah turned her attention back to Esther. "And now you'll go to your reward. You'll be reunited with Sparamizes and your parents and my em too. You'll have no more pain.

"Your son would be here, but you know how men are." Hadassah smiled through tears. "They're strong until they feel helpless. He'd do anything for you, to keep you with him longer. He's king of the most powerful empire in the world, but even he can't stop death."

She sat by her benefactress' bed, dozing and waking to pray the psalms. Longer pauses filled the moments after

Esther's breaths until finally the breaths ceased. Hadassah sat frozen, clinging to Esther's hand until it grew cold.

Benjamin placed his hands on his wife's shoulders, then dried her tears with a scrap of linen. "She's gone, *matok*. It's time to go home to our girls. They need you."

4

When Yael attempted to dismount, her legs refused to support her, and she crumpled to the stones in Tobiah's courtyard. Sore and exhausted, she lay mute and watched as a willowy woman with a pregnancy bump hurried out of the stone house and kissed both Johanan's cheeks. Both jumped when a voice growled from the darkened stable doorway, "I'm hungry, woman. Get me some food."

"Of course, Tobiah," the woman said. "I told the servants to set out bread and fruit before I left the house. Would you like Cook to warm some goat meat or stew?"

"No. We're worn out. Something quick and then to sleep." He nudged Yael with a dirty sandal. "I brought you another servant."

The woman startled, not having seen the pitiful heap in the wavering torchlight. "Is she all right?"

"She's not used to riding," Johanan explained, putting an arm around Yael and hauling her to a standing position. "Mother, this is Yael. Yael, this is my mother Abigail."

Abigail gripped her other arm, and they took her to a small room with shelves full of pots and the scent of spices. Abigail spread a goat's skin on the floor and promised to send water and bread. Yael covered herself with her cloak, worried she'd dropped her bag with all her possessions. Too tired to drag herself out to look for it, she fell into a troubled sleep.

When her aching body wakened her, she ate the bread she found nearby. The scratching of rodents in the storage room's corners stopped when she hissed, "Scat!" She drank to soothe her gritty throat and floated into black oblivion.

The sound of grain hitting the stone floor wakened her. Abigail stood at a tall clay pot, scooping barley into a bowl. "Finally awake," she said with a smile. Setting the bowl on a shelf, she helped Yael rise. "I know walking will hurt, but it will ease the pain in the long run. Do you think you can manage while I carry this?" She retrieved the bowl and ushered Yael down a hall to a kitchen with a hearth and wooden table with stools.

"I don't know if you remember much from last night, but I'm Abigail, wife of Tobiah, mother of Johanan. Once you feel better, you can care for the children. Johanan is my oldest. He has seven younger brothers and sisters...and one on the way as you can see. My daughter Baara who's your age married a moon ago, so you'll be a blessing."

Yael nodded and hobbled to a seat.

"You can call me Cook," said a plump woman with a kind face as she set stew in front of her.

"We don't usually eat anything this heavy in the morning," Abigail continued, "but I knew the men would be hungry."

Ravenous, Yael took a piece of unleavened bread from the platter in the center of the table and scooped stew into her mouth.

"Johanan's already left to check on our goats," Abigail said. "His younger brother Lot and four servants have been

18

pasturing them east of the city. I hope he doesn't have trouble finding them." She gestured to a corner. "He brought your bag in for you."

Yael nodded her thanks.

"Have some more. Traveling builds an appetite," Cook encouraged.

After Yael ate her fill and washed out her bowl, Abigail said gently, "So can you tell me a bit about yourself? I understand you'll be here until the grape harvest."

Heartened that Abigail had been told her stay would be brief, Yael agreed. "Yes, my family owes yours money. We'll have it after the harvest." *Please, Adonai, may it be so.* "Until then I'll serve you to the best of my ability." She stretched her legs.

"You should feel less stiff in a few days, and I'm sure you'll be back to normal next week. Until then we'll show you how we manage our house here in town. Sometimes we travel with the goats, but since this baby is coming a couple months before harvest, I'll be here and you can stay with me. Did you know I'm also a Jew? My father is Shecaniah, keeper of the east gate of Jerusalem."

Yael tried not to let surprise show on her face. "I only go to Jerusalem once or twice a year, and we always go in a western gate, so I don't think my family knows him.

"My family owns a vineyard in Gibeon. At least, we thought we owned it until your husband showed up. A couple lived there when my family moved into the deserted part, but they've been gone ever since I can remember."

"The woman who lived there was my husband's sister," Abigail explained.

"Yes, that's what Tobiah said. I didn't know the vineyard belonged to his sister, who ended up divorced. I don't think anyone in my family did. My father and uncle

19

have been working the vineyard for years, and now my betrothed does too."

"The men will work out all the business details."

Yael decided not to mention her father was absent when Tobiah stormed into their lives. "I'm betrothed to a wonderful man named David." Yael looked around the kitchen. "I know how to bake unleavened or leavened bread, carry water, wash clothing, prune vines, and pick grapes."

"Cook takes care of our meals. We'll show you the well next week. It's a bit of a walk. Can you weave or sew?"

"Yes, I'm good at mending and have spun thread. My mother is a rug weaver, so I can weave too. She learned from her mother in Susa."

"Did your family return to Yehud with Rabbi Ezra?"

"Yes. My mother didn't like the vineyard at first, but I think she was starting to like it before I..." Yael faltered and cleared her throat. "I've always loved it, watching the grapes grow and pressing the wine after harvest."

"It's where you belong," Abigail offered.

"Exactly. My betrothed and I have our own little section where we've started some new vines so it will support more people."

Abigail squeezed Yael's hand. "You're going back, dear. Don't lose heart."

5

After offering two lambs for the morning Sabbath sacrifice, Ezra studied the city from the vantage of the temple mount. He could see activity in the market place. When the next family of worshippers brought their turtledoves as an offering, he asked, "Did you see what's happening in the market?"

"Yes, Rabbi, men from Tyre are selling fish," the husband said.

One of the older boys added, "Jews are selling too, cloth and lentils." The mother sent her son a sharp look.

"Did you notice anything else?"

"There's a crowd buying the goods. Some Gentiles, but many Jews," the head of the family said apologetically.

Ezra sighed. "Do they never learn?"

"Learn what?" the youngest girl asked.

"God's law tells us 'Remember the Sabbath day to keep it holy.' When we disobey, Elohim sends us reminders to obey. If we still don't listen, we suffer consequences."

"It's difficult to control commerce without city gates," the father commented.

"Yes, and even more difficult to hang gates without city walls," Ezra said. "It's another matter for prayer. Can you children add a request for strong walls and gates to your daily prayers?"

"Yes, Rabbi," the five chorused in unison.

"Good." Ezra smiled. "Now let's offer your sacrifice."

After the family sacrificed their doves and departed, Ezra returned to his perch to watch the market area and talk to the Almighty. After requesting walls for Jerusalem, he prayed for each of his daughters, their husbands, and his grandchildren. *And for Abigail and Hallel, my Hadassah's girls. Adonai, I would so like to meet them. May they fulfill their names--'father's joy' and 'praise.'*

The letter he received yesterday contained the sad news of Esther's death. Perhaps Hadassah's family could come home. He remembered how he had sent her away eight years ago.

⌘⌘

Ezra had finished his work for the day and hurried back to his chambers on the temple mount. Although Adin married the year before, Hadassah still remained with him, and her company brightened every evening. His girl had mastered simple cooking and was experimenting with lamb dishes more often. They laughed about the failures and ate the successes with gusto.

"*Abba*, we're having company tonight. Hanani has come from Susa," Hadassah greeted him.

When Hanani arrived, Ezra embraced his friend. "*Shalom*, Hanani. What news do you bring?"

22

Hanani handed him a goatskin pouch. "I have letters to you from your kinsmen and from the synagogue in Susa."

"Very well. Let's eat first. I can read them later."

As they ate, Hanani recounted the deaths, marriages, and births among the Jews in Susa.

"How is your brother Nehemiah?" Ezra asked.

"He's still serving as one of the king's cupbearers. He hopes to become chief among them when Fahraz becomes too old to work."

"It's wonderful he has the king's ear. After what happened with Haman, we need friends among the king's counselors. How long will you be in Jerusalem?"

"I'll be leaving as soon as possible. I already delivered the king's directives to Governor Ahzai."

"Do any of the king's decrees affect us?"

Hanani cleared his throat and looked at Hadassah. "None of the decrees should affect you, but he has requested something of your family."

"What is he asking for?" Ezra asked with a sinking feeling.

Hadassah cleared her throat. "He's asking me to return to care for Esther. She's paralyzed on one side of her body."

The pleasure of Hanani's visit slid from Ezra's face. "Ahh, child."

"I'm merely waiting for your reply before I return," Hanani said.

"Yes, time is crucial." Ezra turned to his daughter. "She might be gone before you get there."

With tears springing to her eyes, Hadassah drew in a deep breath. "I have to try."

Ezra nodded. "A request from the king is a polite command. But Esther sent you away so you wouldn't be added to the harem."

"I'm sure he's moved on to younger women," Hadassah said.

Ezra studied his daughter's flawless skin and shining eyes. Her headdress hid her luxurious, wavy hair. Her lithe figure hadn't been marred by childbirth. The pagan king would still desire her. "You have no idea what your beauty does to men, my dear. You look like a much younger maid." He pushed up from the bench. "Excuse me as I go pray."

Ezra escaped with his troubles to the temple. In the growing twilight, he moved toward the east wall to pray. Since no words would come, he lifted his hands and bowed his head.

Gradually, as his heartbeat settled, he heard the sounds around him. Doves cooed. Levites dropped wood as they prepared the altar. His fellow countrymen muttered prayers.

I will take care of your daughter. I love her even more than you. The words were almost audible. Ezra released a pent-up breath and opened his eyes.

All except one worshipper had departed. In the lamplight, a tall, handsome Israelite prayed, his face twisted with emotion. Reminded of his priestly duties, Ezra approached. "Can I help you, son?"

The man's eyes snapped open. "If you can give me a purpose for living, Rabbi."

Ezra recognized the Gibeonite who had deserted his vineyard to escape his past. When he appeared at the temple, Ezra tasked him with finding wood for the sacrifices. "The usual answer about living for the glory of our God isn't enough?"

24

Benjamin shook his head.

"Although your work here at the temple is crucial, it's not enough either," Ezra deduced.

The man's shoulders slumped.

"Come, sit with me on this bench, Benjamin." After they settled themselves, Ezra asked, "Have you thought about starting another family?"

"Yes, but...I can't lose my family again. I wouldn't survive."

"I completely understand. Did you know my infant son died in the Purim battle and my wife shortly after?"

"No, I didn't know. You've never remarried."

"I have my daughters, and my work. I know deep within my soul that this is enough, but you have no children and you're much younger. The Creator has made each of us differently. Your current life isn't enough for you."

Benjamin studied his calloused hands for several long moments before agreeing, "No, it's not. What can I do?"

Ezra waited so long to reply that Benjamin said, "You don't know any more than I do."

"Actually I believe the Almighty just gave me a thought. I'm working it out." *If this man marries my Hadassah, she could safely return to wait on Esther, couldn't she? Surely the king wouldn't harm him. Artaxerxes does have some morals. After all, he was raised by Esther. My daughter is beautiful, like this man's divorced wife. It would be a second marriage for each of them and could work well for both.*

"As I said, I think the Almighty has given me a solution to your dilemma, as well as a problem I have. Hear me out. It may sound far-fetched at first.

"My daughter Hadassah has been requested by the king to return to Susa. His mother, our good Queen Esther, requires care. Of course, the king's wish is our command. My daughter served as Esther's companion before we arrived five years ago. One of the reasons Esther sent her to Yehud was so the king wouldn't add Hadassah to his harem."

Benjamin stiffened beside him. "I can see why the king would want her. She's the most beautiful woman in Jerusalem."

"Ahh, so you know which woman is my daughter?"

Benjamin shifted uncomfortably. "Every man who works here knows who your daughter is."

Ezra sighed. "Yes, but she has no idea the feelings she arouses in men. I've watched their reactions to her since before she even became a woman, and I've had to protect her since her first husband Jedidiah died."

"My Judith wasn't like that. She flaunted her beauty," Benjamin said sadly.

"A change could be good for you."

"What do you mean?"

"You need a wife. Hadassah needs a husband to protect her." Ezra let his words sink in. "What do you think?"

"You're offering me your daughter? To be the son-in-law of Rabbi Ezra." Benjamin looked dazed by his good fortune. "I've spoken to her a few times. She's very pleasant. And modest."

"One more thing. The wedding would need to be this week."

⌘⌘

That conversation was the strangest Ezra ever initiated, but Benjamin married Hadassah and the two left for Susa within the week.

I hope it's a happy union for both of them. How I miss my eldest child!

6

Hanani admired the roses climbing the high stone walls as he entered the compound of his brother Nehemiah's opulent home in Susa. The roomy main house, built of baked bricks, boasted red shutters framing multiple windows.

Brightly painted birds and flowers covered the interior walls of the foyer where his brother grasped his beard in an affectionate greeting. "Your home is amazing, Nehemiah."

Nehemiah ushered him into a spacious room brightened by a wall of windows. "While you were in Jerusalem, King Artaxerxes gave me the lands of a tax collector who tried to cheat him."

Hanani admired the extensive gardens of citrus and pistachio trees at the back of the house.

"The stables and servants' quarters are hidden by the foliage this time of year."

"It's very impressive," Hanani said.

"I'll show you everything after you sample these nuts and fruit." Nehemiah gestured to a small silver table loaded with edibles. "It was all grown on the property."

Hanani reclined on an ivory couch. "What happened to the tax collector and his family?"

"Thrown to the lions, but I persuaded the king to spare the servants."

"Ayy! Was the tax collector actually guilty?"

"I heard much of the evidence against him, and I believe so."

"Good reminder not to cross the king."

"Yes. And thankfully the Almighty has given me favor with the king."

"Do you think he'll ever award you the chief cupbearer's job?"

"That's what I'm working for, but I don't want it at Fahraz's expense. I want him to retire at a ripe old age."

"Instead of ending up in the lion's den or on the gallows."

"I was thinking more like succumbing to a cup of poisoned wine." Nehemiah winced.

"The hazard of your position. It's been several years since someone attempted to taint the king's food or drink."

"This king's a bit kinder than his predecessors. He's ordered fewer executions than his father."

"Why?"

Nehemiah mulled it over as he sipped his wine. "It might be Esther's influence. She reared him from birth."

"You might be right," Hanani agreed. "Whatever the reason, we can be thankful he's a better monarch than most. I know he pays me well to deliver messages, and he gives me a lot of business back and forth to Yehud."

"I wish the king would allow Jerusalem to be rebuilt."

"The temple and some of the houses are in good repair," Hanani said. "And Rabbi Ezra's succeeded in reviving the temple worship. Our countrymen don't gather for all the festivals, but most come for at least one. There isn't enough housing for all of them to come at one time. Many of the buildings lie in ruins, like the walls."

"The walls! It always comes back to the walls. Our people need the walls to rebuild the city. There's not much point to rebuilding a home or business when the Ammonites or Samaritans can swoop down and take what they like," Nehemiah lamented.

"Agreed. But what can we do? I suppose we could send gold to rebuild the walls like our fathers did to rebuild the temple," Hanani mused. "Are you going to take up another collection?"

"I've been praying about what I could do. I believe I should do more."

"What are you going to do?"

"I could oversee building Jerusalem's walls."

Hanani gaped. "You serve the king. He does trust you, but..."

"This is what the Almighty has directed me to do."

"How do you know?"

"I've prayed for my people night and day since you returned two moons ago and told me of their plight. And while I begged God on their behalf, He said, 'I put you there for this time. What are *you* doing?' Then I saw a vision of our city with the walls blackened and broken down." Nehemiah paused. "I told God if He would give me the king's support, I would go to Jerusalem and rebuild the wall."

"What do you know of building things? You've never built anything," Hanani scoffed.

"I'll find someone who does."

Hanani silently considered his brother's extraordinary idea. "You do have the king's trust, but will he allow a rebellious city to rebuild?"

30

"All I can do is ask and leave the rest up to the Almighty."

"But what about becoming chief cupbearer when Fahraz passes on? You can do great good as an advisor to the king. He still asks you for advice, doesn't he?"

"Yes, he asks often, and I did want to advance. I wouldn't plan to stay in Jerusalem permanently, but for now it seems Elohim is leading me there."

"When will you ask about traveling to Jerusalem?"

"I'm praying for the right time. Our king is still distressed about his mother's passing."

7

Yael gazed wide-eyed at the wares offered in the souk of Rabbah.

"It makes Jerusalem's market look like children playing, doesn't it?" Abigail asked.

Yael nodded mutely. Travel-stained fruit vendors from the country jockeyed with families selling their latest crops of barley. Gold merchants from Arabia displayed impossibly heavy necklaces for wealthy customers to peruse. Other traders sold a dizzying variety of goods from wooden utensils to brass lamps. Permanent shops around the open square housed rug and cloth sellers as well as two bakeries.

In one alley, butchers served lamb, pork, and other meats to hordes of servant girls and matrons. The wind blew the odor of blood into the souk. Yael tried to breathe through her mouth under her veil.

Abigail steered them toward the spice sellers. Yael inhaled the pungent aromas of cinnamon and cardamom. "I want you to meet someone, Yael. He shares our heritage."

She entered a well-appointed shop through a heavy wooden door banded in iron. While the merchant waited on a customer purchasing a small Persian rug, Yael wandered through the store, fingering the rugs, finding a few of good quality near the door, but the most expensive, tightly knotted ones stacked at the rear of the store.

"Shalom, Abigail. Are you searching for a rug today?" the proprietor greeted them in a rich bass voice.

"Good day, Dael. No, I came to introduce you to the newest Jew in our community. Yael is serving my family temporarily, until the grape harvest when she'll return to her home in Gibeon."

"Pleased to meet you, Yael. Gibeon is my hometown. My father is Isaak."

Yael beamed. "I know Isaak's family. It's a pleasure to speak with someone from home."

"I haven't been back for many years. What's happening in my home town?"

Yael considered. "Did you know Rabbi Ezra appointed Oren as our teacher?"

"Yes, my relatives have informed me of that development, as well as the names of the new families who came with the rabbi."

"We were one of the new families. My father is Ariel, and my uncle is Gili. We returned to our ancestral vineyard."

Surprise flitted across Dael's face. "I've heard of your family, though I've never met them. How does the harvest look this year?"

"I don't know, sir. I left when the vines were in bud."

"We'll pray it rains."

"Yes." Yael turned her attention to his wares. "You have some beautiful rugs."

"Thank you. I travel to Persia to obtain the best ones."

"My grandmother weaves rugs in Susa. Her name is Artystone."

"I buy from her. She's one of the best weavers I know. Let me show you one of her wavy patterns." He sorted through the stack, flipping up rugs as he searched. "Ah, here it is. And underneath is another of hers."

Yael stroked the wool threads and then flipped two blue and tan rugs to expose the next. Her breath caught. "This must be one of *softa's* too. My mother's done this pattern, for Governor Ahzai. She used slightly different colors. I watched her make it."

Abigail and Dael retreated to give her time to examine the remaining rugs. She recognized two more patterns. As they departed, she said, "Thank you for bringing me, Abigail. It's like a piece of home."

"Dael said you could stop by anytime. When you go to pick up items for Cook, you should have time to visit occasionally."

"I'll definitely do that."

8

Clinging to Benjamin's arm, Hadassah said, "I wish you didn't have to return to Persepolis."

"So do I, but the king will want to inspect the new wall and gardens before all the satraps arrive for *Noruz,*" Benjamin replied.

"I'm glad you completed it before winter trapped you up there in the mountains. It's been a treat to have you home."

"I know. Praise Adonai! I'm glad I could be with you when Esther passed. I know she mothered you, especially after your em died."

Sadness flickered across Hadassah's face, but she said, "And we've been able to spend more time with Abigail and Hallel."

"Yes, it's a blessing the third wall in Persepolis was finished so quickly. The girls change too much every time I go away." Benjamin bounced five-year-old Hallel on his knee. Setting her down, he said, "Girls, go put some dried meat and fruit in my goatskin pouch." As they scampered off, seven-year-old Abigail planted a kiss on his forehead.

"I'm going to miss you all more than you can know," Benjamin sighed, watching his little ones leave the garden courtyard.

"What project do you think the king will have you oversee now?" Hadassah asked.

"I don't know. All the projects in Persepolis are finished, unless he has a new one in mind." Benjamin tucked his wife's head under his chin. "I've been thinking. You've completed your mission here. What would you think about going back to Jerusalem? I'm sure your father would like to meet his granddaughters."

Abba. My sisters. My dearest friend Jarah. "Do you think the king would let us go?"

"I don't know, but I want to go back." Benjamin's words picked up speed. "See my family in Gibeon, worship in the temple, live among God's people."

"Where would we live?"

"I abandoned the vineyard to Ariel and Gili, so I don't know. Maybe Jerusalem. We'd be near your father there."

"How will you ask the king?"

"I should have an opportunity to speak with him while we're on this trip. I don't know if he'll be willing to let you go. He still considers you one of the ornaments of his empire," Benjamin teased. Then he became serious. "It's in Adonai's hands."

"I like the idea of going back to Jerusalem. I'll pray the whole time you're gone, and we'll see what God will do."

9

Nehemiah poured red wine into the king's goblet, a huge golden flute with a bull handle. *God of heaven, grant me favor with the king. I've been praying for months for an opportunity to speak with him. Will today be the day?*

Nehemiah's hand shook slightly. Since Fahraz was attending a family funeral, the palace steward had summoned Nehemiah to come with all haste. Otherwise, Nehemiah would have broken his fast before serving the king.

He entered one of the palace's private chambers, off the columned main hall. The queen reclined beside her husband. Her cupbearer joined him and waited for Nehemiah to present the king's cup first.

Nehemiah sipped the drink, paused, and presented the cup to the king, handle forward. The king grasped it and drank deeply. When the queen accepted her smaller gold flagon, she sipped it daintily.

A third servant offered a gold bowl overflowing with figs and pomegranates to the lounging couple and then backed into the hall. Nehemiah and his counterpart posted themselves along the walls.

The king and queen chatted amiably, but Nehemiah felt the king's gaze. "My dear, why do you think our esteemed servant looks drawn?"

"I'm not sure, my king. What do you detect?"

"This is not an illness." The king beckoned Nehemiah to approach. "Though you've been absent for days. You're distressed about something. This is sadness of heart. Tell us what's wrong."

Nehemiah could barely force an answer through his suddenly parched throat. "My ancestral city, the location of my family's graves, is a wasteland. The gates are burnt, and my countrymen are open to attack."

"Ahhh...Jerusalem. What do you request?"

Suddenly afraid to present a solution, Nehemiah silently pleaded, *God, move the king's heart.* "If it would please you, and I've been a faithful servant, send me to rebuild Jerusalem, the place of my ancestor's graves."

Artaxerxes stroked his beard, "Your service does please me, and I should appoint a new *Tirshatha* to replace Ahzai, but we would miss you. How long would you be gone?"

"I could report to you after two years. Since I haven't seen the damage, it's difficult to say how long it will take for repairs."

"I hate to part with you for that long, but you would make an excellent governor, and my mother would approve of this project, just as she approved of Ezra's mission."

"It's a thoughtful way to honor your mother during this time of mourning," the queen agreed.

The king fell into a long silence, munching thoughtfully on fruit. "It shall be done," he announced suddenly, clapping his hands.

38

Nehemiah bowed. "If it pleases you, could you send letters with me to the governors along my travel route?"

"Yes, and to Asaph to provide wood from the royal forests in order to rebuild." The king gestured to a scribe sitting cross-legged behind his chaise lounge. The man gathered a stack of clay tablets. "Dictate what you want, Nehemiah, and I'll place my seal on it."

10

Yael brushed seven-year-old Noa's hair and sent her to eat. Then she hurried to tidy the children's sleeping mats. As soon as she ate her grain and fruit, she would leave for the *bet 'amma* for the *Peshach* service. It wouldn't be like celebrating with her family at the Jerusalem temple, but it was better than nothing.

Abigail encouraged her to go to the bet 'amma each Sabbath, but Abigail could only attend when Tobiah wasn't around. His frequent absences allowed her to go a couple of times each moon.

But Abigail and Noa could both go today. Since Tobiah was slated to return later in the week, they wouldn't be able to celebrate all seven days, but today Yael would rejoice. She hummed as she brushed the tangles from her own hair. *"I will lift my eyes unto the hills..."*

Yael went to the hearth for some roasted grain. Yesterday the women had cleansed the house of all leaven, but something seemed to be missing from the holy day preparations. Still sleepy, Yael couldn't think what it could be.

Noa bounced into the room before she finished the grain. "We're leaving now. Are you ready?"

Yael hastily swallowed, took a swig of water, and grabbed a handful of dried figs before following the exuberant child.

The bet 'amma in their part of the city was a large, two-story structure. Indoor and outdoor staircases accessed the upstairs gallery reserved for women. A detailed mosaic adorned the first floor where an ornately carved cabinet called an ark sat on a dais in the middle. Yael liked to arrive early to admire the mosaic before the male worshippers blocked her view.

Abigail couldn't be missed for long, so she never arrived early. She often came late, or left early. Today the threesome arrived together and found standing room where Noa could see.

As the gallery and main room filled and overflowed, the crowd sang psalms, including the psalms of ascent traditionally sung by pilgrims approaching Jerusalem. Yael wiped tears from her cheeks, remembering former Passovers with her family in Jerusalem.

The first elder summarized the nine plagues of judgment the Most High sent on Egypt. After each one the congregation said, "But Pharoah's heart was hardened and he did not listen."

Taking a scroll of Scripture from the ark, a younger man read the portion of Moses' Writings explaining the killing of the Passover Lamb and sprinkling its blood on the Israelites' doorposts. The blood protected them from the Death Angel who came during the night and took the firstborn son of every Egyptian. The thousands of deaths boggled Yael's mind.

A third leader read the instructions for the annual celebration of Peshach. Now Yael realized what was missing from the kitchen that morning—the smell of roasted lamb. Wouldn't Abigail's family eat the most important meal of the festival? Yael's attention returned to hear the end of the teaching.

"'Now you shall eat it in this manner: *with* your loins girded, your sandals on your feet, and your staff in your hand; and you shall eat it in haste—it is the LORD's Passover. For I will go through the land of Egypt on that night, and will strike down all the firstborn in the land of Egypt, both man and beast; and against all the gods of Egypt I will execute judgments—I am the LORD. The blood shall be a sign for you on the houses where you live; and when I see the blood I will pass over you, and no plague will befall you to destroy *you* when I strike the land of Egypt.

"'Now this day will be a memorial to you, and you shall celebrate it *as* a feast to the LORD; throughout your generations you are to celebrate it as a permanent ordinance. Seven days you shall eat unleavened bread, but on the first day you shall remove leaven from your houses; for whoever eats anything leavened from the first day until the seventh day, that person shall be cut off from Israel.

"'On the first day you shall have a holy assembly, and *another* holy assembly on the seventh day; no work at all shall be done on them, except what must be eaten by every person, that alone may be prepared by you. You shall also observe the *Feast of* Unleavened Bread, for on this very day I brought your hosts out of the land of Egypt; therefore you shall observe this day throughout your generations as a permanent ordinance. In the first *month*, on the fourteenth day of the month at evening, you shall eat unleavened bread, until the twenty-first day of the month at evening.'"

If I don't eat the roasted lamb and unleavened bread, what will happen to me? I don't think Abigail's going to follow all the traditions. What can I do? Perhaps if I fast, God will see my heart.

Yael smiled woodenly as Abigail paused to talk with other women after the service. Abigail guided the girl toward a matron at the front of the balcony. "Leyla, I'd like to present Yael, daughter of Ariel of Gibeon. Has Dael mentioned her?"

"Yes, of course. It's nice to meet you." Leyla took Yael's cold hands in welcome. "You're freezing child. Nothing but skin and bones, like Dael said. Shouldn't be any trouble at all for us to share our Passover lamb with this one. Can't imagine she eats more than a mouse."

Abigail turned to Yael. "Enjoy your day, dear. Come home before it's dark so you can put the children to bed."

Yael squeaked "thank you" to Abigail's retreating back. *Thank you, Adonai.* Leyla took her arm, and they descended the inner staircase to find Dael.

Yael held one of Dael's infant grandsons while Leyla, her daughters, and her sons' wives finished preparations for a lavish Peshach feast. Twenty family and friends crowded around the feast spread on a special cloth in Dael's courtyard. A five-year-old grandson began with the first question of the ceremony. "Why is this night different from all other nights?"

Yael relaxed in the familiarity of the shared meal and imagined a time when her son would ask the questions, wording them perfectly. She and David would spend weeks teaching him. Abba and em would be so proud of their first grandson.

Leyla embraced her when she sent Yael home with a servant to guide her. "Come back and see us soon. You're always welcome.

11

Judith untangled herself from a sweaty silk covering. She was gasping in the wake of "the dream." It was the same every time. Three-month-old Hen was looking into her eyes as Judith plunged a six-inch blade into her daughter's beating heart. Warm blood spurted onto Judith's hands and tunic.

Then she was running, running out of Gibeon from a mob of men headed by Benjamin. All she wanted was to stop and wash off the sticky blood, but they kept chasing her, bent on stoning her to death. She managed to keep out of reach of the rocks they threw.

As the dream receded, the enormity of her actions washed over her. She had killed her only daughter. She had borne Ctesias only sons.

Deep within, she knew there would never be another daughter, no matter how many times she gave birth. Hen had been perfect, and she had sacrificed her. She should have taken Hen with her on her trek across Yehud when Benjamin divorced her.

But Ctesias wouldn't have accepted me if I'd been carrying my child, would he? And maybe Moloch noticed my sacrifice. I've enjoyed a good life since I arrived in Susa.

Judith rose from her pillows and opened the window to reveal pink touches of dawn. She stroked her belly. She knew she was carrying another babe. She'd missed her bleeding for two months. Her swollen chest and queasy stomach announced her fifth pregnancy. The nausea usually kept her abed late. The dream always came more frequently during a pregnancy.

To ensure a healthy pregnancy, she decided to offer sacrifices to the gods. Later today she would call for a litter and take fruit and flowers to the graves of Ctesias' mother and father. Many Persians, including her husband, followed Zoroastrian rites. Although the Persians didn't worship Moloch, others in this city did, and they had built their god a magnificent temple. She'd stop on her way back from the bone crypt.

First she needed more rest. Keeping her eyes on the comforting tinge of dawn on the horizon, she snuggled back into her pillows.

⌘⌘

Naama positioned the blue and tan Persian rug so she could watch her younger children race up and down the path bisecting the vineyard. The vines wilted from lack of the late rains, so Ariel, Gili, and Raisa were trickling water onto their roots from pots they carried to and from the spring in Gideon. She would be portaging water also, but she needed to finish this rug to redeem her beloved Yael.

"Redeem us from the oppression of men," Naama altered one of the prayers from the Writings to encompass

her whole family. She also repeated the promise Jarah had taught her: *"The Lord redeems the soul of His servants, and none of those who take refuge in Him will be condemned."* Tobiah snatched Yael three moons ago. *How is she, Lord? Is she well? I miss her.*

Lost in her musings, Naama didn't notice Tova's approach. "Eliezer wanted to water your vines, so we carried over a couple of pots."

"Thank you. He's very kind."

"Every year in the month of his birth, I tell him the story of how you brought him into the world and got him to breathe. Judith wouldn't have known what to do, and I would have lost him. He knows he owes you his life."

Naama smiled. "Elohim gave him life."

"Elohim used your hands," Tova insisted.

"I'm glad I knew what to do. I saw my em and softa deal with several difficult births. The results weren't always so happy."

"We'll do anything we can to help you get Yael back. We have five pieces of silver to contribute. Menachem says they're yours, late payment for midwifing our babies."

Overwhelmed, Naama couldn't speak, so she bent over her project and knotted an area of tan threads. "That means so much," she whispered.

She cleared her throat and looked up at her friend. "What do you know of Tobiah? You must know something about him, since you were friends with Judith in Rabbah."

Tova's face drained of color.

"Please, Tova."

"He was kinder to his sister than my brother was to me," she offered.

Naama remembered Tova's brother had offered his unwanted child to Molech after impregnating one of the

46

servants. The comparison failed to cheer Naama. "Was Tobiah kind to you?"

"No. He teased me unmercifully, or ignored me."

"How did he treat the family servants?"

"I never saw him acting cruel. He seemed to be very good to his first wife. He hadn't taken other wives before I left."

"How many does he have?"

"He married twice, but one died. Abigail, daughter of Shecaniah the gatekeeper, is the surviving wife. Her family would know more about him."

Realizing Tova's discomfort, Naama said, "Have you heard when Jarah's family will return from Jerusalem?"

"Any day now. I'll bring her out to the vineyard as soon as she catches up on her housework in Gibeon. We'll bring more water."

⌘⌘

Yael showed Noa how to make thread with a hand spindle. Since Noa was tall and coordinated, she managed the spindle well, but Yael saw the longing in her eyes when Johanan entered the courtyard and scooped up toddler Shobi. She took the spindle from her young student to finish the spool.

After speaking with his younger siblings, Johanan sat on a rock beside her while five-year-old Hymie ran to fetch cold water. "You're looking better than the last time I saw you."

"I can stand on my own," Yael replied with a smile. "Only took a few days for the soreness to subside."

"Have you ridden one of the Arabians since?"

"No!"

Johanan laughed. "You should take short rides so you'll be ready for longer ones." He whistled and his chestnut cantered over. He rubbed her muzzle. "Do you want to ride her while I step inside? I'm headed back out to the goats but thought I'd check in here after I went to the market. How's my mother?"

"She seems to be carrying the baby well. She's often tired." Yael regarded the mare with distaste.

"She calls you a godsend."

"I hardly think God sent me here."

"Don't you believe He controls everything?"

"Yes, but I believe people make choices too, and He doesn't always stop them."

"I think He uses people's choices for His own ends, Yael. You'll see. This isn't the end."

Yael grunted as she gripped a chunk of mane and mounted from a rock.

"Are you worried about not being able to return home?"

"Wouldn't you be, if you were me?"

Johanan considered. "Don't you think your family will have thirteen coins after harvest?"

"They should, but I'm not sure how they'll have forty. Like you, I have younger siblings. They need shelter." She nudged the horse away from its master toward the far end of the courtyard.

Hymie handed Johanan a clay cup of water and climbed into his lap. When Johanan sent him back to the kitchen to return the cup, Yael guided the horse back to Johanan and slid off.

"My father and I are traveling to Jerusalem in three moons. I'm taking Meshullam's daughter as my bride. I'll ask if you can come as an escort for my new wife."

48

"Since the baby will be born by then, I might be able to." She considered the possibility of seeing familiar territory, including the temple. "Thank you," she added with growing excitement.

"You should ride at least every other day, or you'll end up as sore as you were after our first trip. There's a gray nag reserved for the children. She'd be a good mount to take you on errands." He rose. "I need to be on my way so I make camp by nightfall. Shalom, Yael."

"Shalom, Johanan. And thank you again."

"Don't be too hasty with your thanks. We don't have my mother's permission yet," he answered as Yael opened the gate and he cantered onto the street.

12

I f it pleases the king, I'll leave in the middle of Iyar,"
Nehemiah said.

"It pleases the king," Artaxerxes said. "You have all the
letters of instruction to the governors?"

"Yes."

"I'm also sending a contingent of cavalry with you.
They'll stay in Jerusalem so one of the units there can
return to Susa. How many servants are you taking?"

"Twenty. Some of them have families."

"What of your mother?"

"She'll stay and oversee my property here. I'm leaving
my chief steward here as well."

"A good plan. You've been faithful with the property
I've given you and honest in paying your taxes. Build a fine
governor's mansion in Jerusalem after you finish the walls.
I will notify Tirshatha Ahzai, to return to Susa."

"Thank you, Magnificent." Nehemiah bowed, grateful
not to deal with a potentially disgruntled ex-governor. He
began to back out of the apadana.

"I almost forgot. I'm also sending the family of Benjamin the Gibeonite with you. His wife served my mother well, and they desire to return to their homeland. They have two small daughters, but I'll see that they're properly mounted so they don't slow you down."

"I'll enjoy their company."

"I will miss your service here. Go with your God, Nehemiah."

⌘⌘

Benjamin sauntered down the main thoroughfare in Susa's merchant sector. He peered into shops of jewelry, cloth, spices, and housewares. Athenian black pottery caught his eye, and he entered a prosperous-looking storefront. Perhaps he could afford a small piece for his mother.

A Parthian armed with a curved sword stood guard near the door. At the sound of the door, the proprietress emerged from a back room. When he greeted her, both froze.

Benjamin felt his face flush. He was furious...and relieved at the same time. Furious about the murder of his darling Hen, relieved that the woman he'd protected as his own flesh and blood survived their divorce and her banishment. After a protracted pause, he choked out, "Judith, how did you end up here?"

"By marrying well," she answered shortly.

"I see," Benjamin said slowly, taking in her expensive silk robes and gold jewelry. "You're looking as elegant as always."

"I don't usually mind the family shop, but my husband Ctesias is away on business and his assistant is in bed with a fever. I like selling the expensive pieces, and my husband says at least I won't cheat him."

"It's important for a husband to trust his wife."

Discomfited, Judith turned to fiddle with a display of pottery. "You're a long way from Gibeon."

"My wife served the king's mother."

"I heard she passed on?"

"Yes, and now we're returning home, which is the reason I'm here. I wanted to purchase something for my mother. I doubt she's ever seen this fine black pottery. Do you have some pieces...without figures on them?" Benjamin asked, struggling to remain coherent.

"Ah, yes, Jews don't purchase the ones with figures because the images could be considered idolatrous," Judith said, a touch of derision in her tone. She softened, "Some are primarily black. They're not priced as high because they lack the detail of the pottery with figures. Look around and tell me what you decide." Trembling, she disappeared behind a scarlet cloth into the back room.

Judith collapsed on a stool in the crowded storeroom. *Perhaps the gods heard my petitions and sent this opportunity for me to right the wrong I've done Benjamin. Usually fathers choose the sacrifices to Moloch. Sometimes the mothers agree. Sometimes they don't, but in Hen's case, I alone made the decision.*

Judith patted her cheeks and sipped some water. She grabbed the closest pot and reemerged into the front room.

When she appeared with a huge jar of pungent cinnamon, Benjamin approached with a small bowl.

"Your mother deserves better than *that*."

"I know, but she'll appreciate even this."

Judith turned to a display of large pieces and found a matching platter. "I'd like to send a gift to your mother. She was always kind to me, but I caused her pain." She began wrapping both dishes in goatskin.

52

"This is a costly gift."

"Yes, to atone for a costly error," she said, pausing to regard him steadily.

"Thank you. I can imagine her serving our Peshach lamb on it."

"So can I," Judith took a huge breath. "Benjamin, I'm sorry...about Hen."

Some of Benjamin's rage leaked away, but the question that had haunted him for years surfaced. "How could you...?" he choked, unable to continue.

Judith dropped her eyes to the floor. "I was raised differently, Benjamin. I was being forced to make a new start, and I needed Moloch's blessing, so I brought him a sacrifice." Her voice sunk to a whisper. "And I was so angry that you'd send us away."

"I didn't want to. I'd decided to take you and Hen to your family in Rabbah so you'd be safe, but Tova found me before the caravan left. Menachem and I went to the high place. I was mad with grief after I saw... I don't remember what happened for days. Later, Dael sent a message he'd found you injured, but you disappeared."

Judith ducked her head, ashamed of how she'd taken advantage of Dael. "I found my new life on the journey," she whispered.

"Judith, I *am* glad you're safe. I'm sorry for the pain we caused each other. I didn't know Jews weren't supposed to marry Ammonites until Ezra read the scroll and decreed the divorces. I wish you'd come to call the God of Israel your own."

When Judith failed to respond, he continued, "Only Adonai can forgive us both, Judith, but for what it's worth, I forgive you."

She smiled slightly.

"Adonai has blessed me with two more daughters."

"I have four sons," she said.

"That's good."

"Is there anything else I can do...to make things right?"

"Turn to the one true God."

Judith handed him the wrapped purchases. "Go with your God, Benjamin."

"Peace be on you and yours." Benjamin strode out of the shop, parcel under one arm, free of a burden he hadn't realized he carried.

13

Naama listened to the patter of rain on the plaster roof. *Praise Adonai!* The rain was late, but much needed. She continued knotting tan wool threads while eying Raisa's progress with the lentil stew, which would feed the family for three or four days. "Give it another stir."

"Yes, Em," Raisa said, rising from the floor where she entertained Ebin with wooden blocks. "Em, you'd better come look at this."

Naama put aside the two-thirds finished rug. "What is it?"

As she reached her daughter, who was looking at the low ceiling, they heard a rumbling. Pushing Raisa toward Ebin, Naama snatched the cooking pot and stepped back as wet branches and plaster tumbled onto the hearth.

"Grab Ebin and go in the bed chamber," she yelled at Raisa, who stood frozen in the middle of the room. Raisa whirled and grabbed the toddler who was screaming lustily.

"Saul, come quick!" Raisa called as she ran out the door.

Registering the heat from the pot, Naama hastily set it down. She wrapped it in her headdress, ran to the door and set it in the courtyard, before dashing back to snatch her rug and threads from the wooden table.

Raisa reappeared. "Quick, get the stools from this end of the room," Naama gestured as she ran toward the ruins and filled the front of her robe with small kitchen utensils and bread, glancing nervously at the ceiling above her. As she dropped them in the courtyard, another chunk of ceiling fell with a thud.

"Stay out of the room now," Naama shouted to Raisa. "I don't know how much will fall. Let's carry all this into the bed chamber. Wait—let me look at the ceiling first."

She gazed at the stick and mud ceiling. *It looks sound, but should I shelter the children and our things in here or brave the open courtyard? Better to be soaked and safe.*

She shooed all the children out into the rain. Saul tried to shield Ebin with his taller body, and Naama and Raisa huddled around Nasha, who had returned to the house from tending their goats.

"Naama! What happened?" Ariel and David ran into the courtyard, grabbing what she'd salvaged and herding the family into the storage space across from the kitchen.

"Part of the kitchen roof collapsed. I didn't know if we'd be safe in any of the other rooms."

The men scanned the ceiling. "It looks sound," David said.

Ariel scooped up the crying Ebin and went to investigate. "The bed chamber ceiling is fine," he announced when he returned. "Being there will be more comfortable than sitting here with the grain and oil. I think this storm's going to last a while. Come, children."

Naama found dry robes and blankets for everyone. "You were all very brave and obedient," she said, rubbing Nasha's sopping hair with a rag.

56

Ariel passed Ebin to David and drew his wife close. "I was waiting until after harvest to replace the kitchen roof. I'm so sorry, Naama. Are you hurt?"

"Well, I..." Naama noticed a pain in her hands and held them up. "I burnt my hands saving the lentils."

"Let's get cold water on them. Raisa, get the ointment and some cloth." Ariel led her to one of the small windows and unlatched it. "Here hold them in the rain, matok. Do they hurt much?"

"I didn't notice them before, but yes, they hurt."

"I'm glad no one was hurt worse."

"Me too. Raisa noticed something was wrong, so we had a little time to react."

"It looks like you got most everything out," David announced, returning from a trip to check on the kitchen. "Do you want to try to get the table?"

"No. Wait until the rain passes. It will stop soon enough."

Ariel took the cooling ointment and gently applied it to his wife's burns. "You're going to have to take a break from your rug."

"Oh, no, Ariel! I hadn't thought of that," Naama wailed.

"Shh," Ariel soothed, discreetly nodding toward their frightened children.

Naama took a deep breath. "I *need* to finish it," she insisted softly.

"Let's see how your fingers are in the morning, matok." He hugged her. "And let's remember to be thankful the ceiling didn't land on anyone."

Naama's eyes filled with tears, and she burrowed into her husband's strong shoulder to hide them.

14

Hadassah watched her five-year-old daughter hold the reins of Nehemiah's Arabian as he guided their mount. Since Hallel was too young to ride by herself, she rode with an adult, switching at each rest stop. Her favorite companion was Nehemiah.

Although their leader had no children, a crowd of youngsters instantly surrounded him each night as they set up camp. *How will he govern Yehud with a pack of children following him? A pity he has none of his own, but, like many of the king's servants, he never married.*

Hadassah's attention turned to Benjamin, who rode beside her with seven-year-old Rachel in his arms. They exchanged amused looks. "I think our next stop will be sooner than usual," Benjamin said.

Hadassah laughed. "You think our Hallel is more tiring than the king?"

"Don't you?"

"You just might be right."

Hadassah's heart sang, full of family joy. These three were so precious. She longed for one more, a boy. Maybe once they were settled, but they still didn't know where they would live. Hopefully near Abba in Jerusalem. He deserved to spend time with his granddaughters.

When Rachel started to get restless, begging to get down and run, Hadassah said, "We're blessed to have horses to ride. Did you know I walked this whole way the first time I came to Yehud? It took five moons."

Rachel's eyes widened.

"I came with your grandfather and my three sisters. You're going to meet them as soon as we get to Jerusalem. You'll also get to meet the friend I made on that trip. Her name is Jarah, and she has four boys. One of them is your age."

"What's his name?"

"Doran. I can't wait to meet him and her youngest son Gedalya. I haven't seen her for eight years. And I can't wait to introduce you and Hallel to my friend."

This is so different from my last trek from Susa to Yehud. Then she had been newly widowed, childless. Worse, she had felt forgotten by God, but that wasn't the truth. Since emotions flowed high and low, you couldn't trust them. But you could trust God—the God who had written her on the palms of His hands, according to the Scriptures Jarah had taught her. Jarah was an orphan, so she had understood Hadassah's feelings.

Jarah would envy the ease of this trip. Laughter bubbled up as she thought of Jarah astride one of these horses. Her hefty friend had never ridden and would have disliked the jouncing. *Truth be told, I'm tired of it too.* Hadassah shifted her weight and gladly welcomed the break Nehemiah called before midday.

Benjamin winked at her as they dismounted.

15

Judith stepped carefully. Her protruding abdomen made her clumsy on the polished marble stairs. She should move her bedchamber to the first floor, so she wouldn't have to negotiate the steps, but it was noisier and her pregnancy already made it hard to sleep.

"Sasha, I need you to move my things to the empty bed chamber downstairs," Judith told the maid who followed her with a large fan.

A racket drew her attention as Ctesias' oldest son Oibares vaulted down the stairs carrying a heavy urn. The tall urn obstructed his vision, and Judith shrieked as the heavy pottery clipped her. Losing her balance she rolled down the stairs. Splayed face down on the unyielding stone floor, she moaned.

"Are you all right?" Sasha asked.

Oibares leaned over her. "Catch your breath and I'll help you up."

Rolling to her side, she caught him smirking before she grimaced in pain and a rush of fluid soaked her legs. "Merciful Moloch, not now. The baby will never survive."

Oibares yelled for more servants as Judith's world became spotty and then black.

60

As the haze began to recede, she heard someone say, "Fetch the doctor. She's going to need more expertise than I have."

Judith struggled to focus. "My... my babe?"

"We're going to do all we can. Drink a little of this for the pain," the voice soothed. Judith tasted blood on her lip. A damp cloth caressed her face. "You're a sight, but you're going to be all right." The knifing pangs in her gut told her the baby wasn't. She surrendered to oblivion with the next contraction.

When Judith woke, her flaccid stomach was a grim testament to all she'd lost.

A Persian woman emerged from the corner of the room. Judith remembered her voice asking for the physician. "I'm Artystone. I have training as a midwife. Would you like to see your little girl's body? It comforts some mothers."

A girl? But I knew I'd never have a girl.

This one isn't alive, is she?

The woman with the sympathetic manner was waiting patiently for an answer. *Do I want to see this baby?* "I...yes...I'd like to see her."

The little girl was impossibly tiny, but every feature was formed. She had ten fingers and ten toes and curled inward as if she were still safely inside Judith's womb.

Judith sobbed, and a searing sense of guilt stole her breath. She had angered one of the gods. Otherwise this never would have happened. She must make things right, but first she had to figure out whom she'd offended.

She handed the baby gently back to Artystone. "Thank you."

"I'm so sorry for this loss. Rest now."

Judith nodded and closed her eyes so she could think. *I gave Hen to Moloch, and he blessed me for years. I've followed all the rites to Ahura Mazda. Who else could I have offended? Must be the God of Israel, Benjamin's god. Apologizing to Benjamin wasn't enough. How can I make things right? The Jewish God has only one temple, and it's in Jerusalem.*

Too tired to come up with an answer, Judith drifted to sleep.

16

Judith watched her youngest son play in the walled garden with a teenaged servant. He exhibited good coordination for a four-year-old. "Em, watch!" he shouted as he threw a ball. The servant girl gently threw it back, and he caught it easily.

"Well done!" Judith praised the dark-haired imp.

He became involved in the game and forgot about his mother. She shifted on the stone bench, trying to ease the ribs the physician said were cracked, and wondering how she could make amends with the God of the Jews. There were one or two bet 'ammas in Susa, but she wouldn't be welcomed at these houses of worship.

She needed to go to Jerusalem and offer a sacrifice in the temple. Ctesias's caravans went all the time. Now to figure out how to get him to let her go. She could guilt him into it. Oibares had purposely run into her on the stairs. She could tell from the expression on his face when he offered to help her up. His mother had probably put him up to it.

Ctesias' first wife had been jealous of her since she arrived twelve years ago, but that woman was as drab as mud. Judith had taken over the household and Ctesias' heart.

Oibares had been born while Ctesias was away on the trip on which he found Judith. His mother had steeped him in hate, and the boy, named for Ctesias' father, had always been insolent to Judith. Ctesias doted on him, but wouldn't ignore this incident. He had been disappointed about the baby's death, even though she was a girl.

⌘⌘

Ctesias joined her in her bed chamber that evening. "How are you feeling, my jewel?"

"Better. Not back to normal yet, but much improved," Judith tried to smile at him.

"I'd like to have you examined by the physician."

"Could the midwife come instead? Her kindness and wisdom were a comfort to me."

Ctesias thought briefly. "That should be fine. Send a servant to get her this week. She might not be able to come right away if she's midwifing. The rest of the time she weaves rugs."

"That's a strange combination."

"She received her training from her mother, who attended the palace harem, so she's an excellent midwife. Her craft is the rugs. Maybe you should order a rug for your room while she's here."

"I'd like that! What a generous husband you are," Judith flattered. Rug weaving and midwifery niggled at the edges of her memory. She decided to wait to broach her request.

64

Two weeks later Ctesias came to her room again.

"Come in, darling. The midwife says I'm back to rights." He joined her on the bed. Moving her hands sensuously, she stroked his thick hair as he lay in her lap. "She did think it would be prudent to ensure the safe arrival of our next child."

Ctesias moaned. "How would we do that? Can we start creating one now?"

Judith gave a throaty laugh. "Not quite yet, but I'll take good care of you tonight, love. It seems I may have angered Adonai."

"The god of the Jews? How do you figure that?"

"Well, I've been careful to please Moloch and Ahura Mazda, but Adonai could be upset about something I did before I met you."

Ctesias relaxed. "So how do we appease him?"

"This is the hard part. There's only one temple..."

"And it's in Jerusalem," Ctesias finished.

"Yes, I'd like to offer a sacrifice."

"I'm leading a caravan that way soon. I can send an offering of whatever animal you like."

"It might be more complicated. What I did is abhorrent to the Jews' god," Judith admitted.

"What *did* you do?"

In the ensuing silence, water pinged into a brass bowl. "I sacrificed my first-born to Moloch."

"The Jews don't sacrifice their children?"

"No. It's punishable by stoning."

Ctesias pulled his head from her lap and looked into her eyes. "Was that why you weren't traveling in the caravan the day I found you?"

"Yes, the Gibeonites were hunting for me."

"Ahh," Ctesias paused. "It seems like Moloch heard your prayers. I found you and brought you here."

"Yes, but it's the only offense I can think of." She placed her hand on his thigh.

Ctesias struggled to think. "So you want to go to Jerusalem? Would you be safe there?"

"I think so. I don't have to tell anyone why I'm making the sacrifice. They won't let me beyond the outer court of their temple anyway."

She continued moving her hands in ways Ctesias most liked.

Ctesias moaned. "I like having you around. It will be a pleasure taking you on my next trip. Extra guards will keep you safe."

17

Grateful for Johanan's advice to ride regularly, Yael cantered up to Jerusalem with his wedding group. Besides Johanan's seven-year-old sister Noa, she was the only female.

Her heart sang as the buildings of Jerusalem rose on Mount Moriah. *I will lift my eyes unto the hills from where my help comes. My help comes from the Lord, the Maker of heaven and earth.*

As she strained to glimpse the temple, she noticed clouds of dust from activity around the city.

"What are they doing?" Johanan asked her. "It's not one of the holy days, is it?"

"No. I have no idea what's going on, but I'm so glad to be here. Thank you again."

"You'll help Eden adjust and see to her needs. No need to thank me." Johanan urged his chestnut to catch up with his father at the head of the entourage.

"What are these Jews doing?" Tobiah cried as they approached. "Let's go around to Shecaniah's gate. We won't have any trouble there."

Shecaniah greeted his family warmly. "Come to collect your bride, my boy? Mazel tov!"

"Yes, yes. Johanan's come for Meshullam's daughter. But what's all the activity at the wall?" Tobiah asked impatiently.

Shecaniah straightened. "Our new Tirshatha arrived from Susa. A godly Jew named Nehemiah. Hadn't been here a week before he brought up the idea of rebuilding our walls. He's got the support of the priests, merchants, and common folk. Everyone pitched in and has been working hard."

Tobiah looked disgusted. "Have you prepared rooms for the servants?"

"Absolutely. Everything's ready. They can make themselves comfortable. You're welcome to stay too."

"We have accommodations closer to the bride's family. One of Meshullam's friends is hosting us," Tobiah said.

"Of course. Meshullam is well-connected."

"Mother sends her greetings, Grandfather. You have another fine grandson, as of a moon ago," Johanan added.

"Praise Adonai! What's the little fellow's name?"

"Nahash." Tobiah drew himself erect on his horse.

"I'll send a gift back with you. Is there anything Abigail wants?"

"Nothing you can get her," Tobiah mumbled.

Johanan spoke quickly to cover his father's rudeness. "She'd love some Judean honey."

"Right. She always liked a bit of sweetness with her bread. I'll get her some. See you at the marriage feast."

"Be sure you clean up before you arrive," Tobiah muttered as the riders entered his father-in-law's gate.

After leaving Noa and all of the servants except for a stable boy and Yael at Shecaniah's house, the small party continued toward the Fish Gate and the home of Meshullam.

68

Yael was surprised when Meshullam's wife answered the door. *Doesn't the family have a servant?*

"Shalom, shalom," the plump woman said. "I'll send word immediately to Meshullam. He and the servants are busy on the wall across the street. Such bad timing for a wedding, I told him, but he said life goes on. It's time Eden was married and settled." She ushered them into a foyer with cushioned benches. "Eden, come greet your betrothed and go tell your father he's arrived."

A slim, elegantly robed girl answered her mother's call. "Shalom, Johanan. Shalom, Tobiah. If you'll excuse me, I'll get Abba while Em gets cold drinks."

Before her mother had time to serve the wine, Eden returned with an older, male version of herself. Meshullam greeted his guests with polite formality and sent his daughter to assist her mother.

When he noticed Yael standing in a corner, he told her to go down the hall and find the other women. Yael followed the excited voice of the mistress of the house past several doorways to a large kitchen

"I'm Yael, daughter of Ariel of Gibeon. I'm serving Tobiah's family temporarily."

"It's wonderful to meet you, Yael. I'm glad they brought a woman along for Eden. She's never been on such a long trip before, although she rides beautifully. Now take a cup for yourself, and if you could take this one out to the stable hand. Let him know you'll be going back down the street to the high priest's home just as soon as your group has been greeted and refreshed."

Feeling like she'd been caught in a whirlwind, Yael delivered the message and lingered outside to collect her thoughts and breathe in the air of Jerusalem. Thrilled to see the temple close by, she vowed to find time to slip away and pray. She wished she had a dove to offer.

Yael turned her attention to the wall where two burly servants worked across the street from Meshullam's two-story home. On their way from the east gate, they had passed several groups of laborers, and she could see a group working farther down the wall.

It would be good to have walls around Jerusalem again. Her em's friend Jarah always talked about how the city needed her walls. Jarah made Jerusalem sound *alive*, bereft without protection. Truth be told, she was a lot like Eden's lively and warm-hearted em.

Yael found a seat in the shade. Meshullam and his guests exited his home before she could drink in all the sights on the busy street. Taking their horses by their reins, they retraced their steps and stopped in front of the most impressive edifice on the street.

"This is the home of Eliashib, the high priest," Meshullam explained. "He's busy supervising work on the wall, but will meet you this evening. You'll have time to rest and freshen up. After the evening sacrifice, we'll share a meal here and talk over plans for the week."

A pleasant-faced, older woman answered Meshullam's knock and offered them water for washing, before going to fetch her mistress.

Elizabeth swept into the room in a cloud of perfume and sky-blue silk. "Bring fruit and bread," she told the servant.

"Come, recline," she invited her guests. "I'm pleased to meet you, Tobiah. And this must be Johanan. I've heard much about you from Eden."

"Thank you for hosting us," Tobiah answered as he settled himself. "Our servant took the horses around back. Will there be someone to show him where to stable them?"

70

"Yes, my husband left one of the boys to clean up and settle your horses in. All the other male servants are toiling on the Tirshatha's wall. I can't imagine how long the project will take, but it's rather inconvenient."

"Tirshatha Nehemiah hasn't estimated when it will be finished?" Tobiah asked.

"Not that I've heard. It's such a mess from being demolished in King Zedekiah's day that I imagine it will take several moons. Everyone's slaving on it now, but some of the farmers and vinedressers will need to harvest their crops soon. Jews have come from all over Yehud to rebuild."

"It's good to have widespread support for such a large project," Johanan said, when his father failed to answer. "My sister Noa will arrive shortly. We left her with her grandfather Shecaniah while we got settled. And this is Yael, who will assist my bride as we travel back to Rabbah. As you know, my mother recently gave birth. Although she and the baby are well, she couldn't travel this soon."

"I'm pleased to meet you, Yael," Elizabeth said. She turned her attention to the men, "We have two rooms prepared for your family. Your servant can bunk with ours. Several of our other rooms are occupied by those working on the wall, but your rooms are large so you should be quite comfortable."

"Your home is impressive," Tobiah answered. "I'm sure we'll be very comfortable."

18

Yael slipped away after eating in the kitchen with the other servants. *What a relief to be served only approved foods!*

At Tobiah's she tried to figure out the ingredients in each dish, so she wouldn't eat any unclean foods like pork. Some nights she ate only bread. It was plain food, but it was enough.

Tonight they had eaten lamb with herbs, and leavened bread. The familiar food made her miss home.

The temple was a short walk from the high priest's home. As she entered the women's court, she admired the carvings of the Shushan gate. According to her *abba*, it depicted the Persian capitol of Susa in honor of King Cyrus, who commissioned the rebuilding of the temple. Susa looked like a beautiful city.

Her father said Jerusalem was striking in its days under King Solomon when gold covered the temple, but had declined and been destroyed by King Nebuchadnezzar because of the Jews' disobedience.

Yael paused for the ceremonial washing and headed for a corner of the courtyard to get her bearings. Tears threatened as she watched a family of seven bring their lamb for sacrifice. If her family worshipped at the temple recently, there were only six of them. Two-year-old Ebin was old enough for the trip. Had she missed his first trip since his circumcision? Would her baby brother even remember her?

She prayed and soaked up the peace, lingering until the sun began to disappear. This visit would have to last at least two more moons until she could return home. She hadn't seen any worshippers bringing first fruits offerings of grapes. Was the harvest good this year? She'd ask the vendors in the market.

When she returned to Eliashib's, Eden joined her in the bedchamber she shared with Noa. "The wedding ceremony's been set for the day after tomorrow. After three nights of feasting, we'll leave early for Rabbah. Johanan said it will take about three days to reach the city. We'll spend a moon there before we go out with the herds.

"Will you help me get accustomed to the mount Johanan brought me? I saw her in the stable, and I'm not as good a rider as my em thinks. I've never ridden such a fine horse. Usually I ride an older, gentle mare."

"Tomorrow morning we'll get you up on her and pick up a few things for Abigail at the market. At least you've ridden before. My first ride lasted for hours, and by the time we reached Rabbah I couldn't walk. Johanan practically carried me into the house."

At the flash in Eden's eyes, Yael added hastily, "Abigail supported me on one side and Johanan on the other. I fell asleep as soon as they deposited me on the floor of the storage room."

"Is that where you sleep?"

"No, I only slept there the first night. I stay close to the little ones and take care of them, so Abigail can tend the baby at night. They're wiggly, and they snore, but I have my own pallet, and I'm used to it because I'm the oldest of four."

"I'm the youngest of six."

"Your mother will miss you when you're gone," Yael said with a pang of homesickness for her em.

"Johanan's promised to visit at least once a year. His father comes often."

"He's a very considerate man--Johanan, not Tobiah." Eden's brow furrowed, so Yael plunged on with her next thought, "The visits will only work when you're not pregnant or caring for a little one."

At Eden's look of dismay, Yael wished she'd kept quiet.

19

From the roof of the governor's house, Nehemiah stretched aching muscles unused to physical labor as he watched the stars appear. He held up his roughened hands and surveyed the cuts. They'd callous soon. It would take a long time after the wall's completion before they would return to their former manicured softness so he could serve the king.

He could simply supervise, but he believed men should lead by example. As it was, any one of the sturdy Jews could outwork him. They'd just never had the vision or the leadership to rebuild the walls.

Nehemiah missed court life. This was important work, but Jerusalem was a backwater. He didn't know what was happening in Susa or Damascus or Thebes or any of the other seats of power. A little news trickled in with the caravans, but not much.

His home in Susa was more elaborate than this governor's mansion. The king had commissioned fine timber to expand and beautify the Jewish residence, but it lacked land and gardens, and a bathing area. A hot bath would ease his screaming muscles.

He missed hearing the problems of the empire while Artaxerxes consulted with his vizier and other advisors. He had tried to think of fair solutions so if the king asked, he could offer wise counsel. Often the king discussed issues with him and asked for his input. His advice saved several subjects from execution after he convinced the king the evidence against them was insufficient.

Who is the king confiding in now? Will he listen to me when I return?

20

When Eden arrived at Eliashib's stables the next day, Yael helped her mount the gray filly Johanan had given her as a bride gift.

"She's still docile because of the long trip, so I'm sure you'll do fine. Guide her with pressure from your knees. She won't know the streets like your horse does." Yael climbed on her small bay and led the way out the gate.

"Will she spook?" Eden asked as they walked their horses side by side toward the East Gate.

"Possibly. She's used to wide open spaces, but she's been ridden in Rabbah a few times."

"What's Rabbah like?"

"It's bigger than Jerusalem, more sophisticated because it's on a major trade route. I'm told it snows a few times every winter."

"Ohhh, I can't wait. I've only seen snow a few times."

"They bring the herds down from the mountains when it gets cold.

"You'll need to be more careful in the city. It's not as safe. People are more pushy, bolder. It even feels a little...wicked. There are temples to several gods. A lot of temple prostitutes. There are parts of the city you need to stay away from."

Eden shivered. "Does Abigail run her home like ours, or is it different since Tobiah's Ammonite?"

"They don't follow the law's dietary restrictions. Have you thought about how you'll handle that?"

"I'm going to follow our people's cooking customs. I'm surprised Abigail doesn't follow them."

Yael ignored the criticism of her mistress. "She's a good woman, kind. Her younger boys aren't circumcised though. I'm not sure about Johanan."

Eden thought a moment. "I didn't consider that. It will distress abba if his grandsons aren't. Maybe Johanan would be willing to have them circumcised."

"It might be a good idea to have your father bring it up before the wedding."

"Do you think it would be a problem?"

"For Johanan, probably not. For Tobiah, who knows? He takes offense easily."

"Yes, I already know about his touchiness. He was trying to arrange a marriage for Johanan with one of Zadok's daughters, but it fell through for some reason. Maybe the bride price. Johanan offered limestone for me, but abba has to find a way to transport it. Abba doesn't need it but will donate it to rebuild Jerusalem. Even before the wall was started, abba knew a lot of the houses could use new stone."

"Some of them are ruins."

"Yes, many spots need to be cleared completely. They're using some of the rubble in the walls."

"Wouldn't it be better to use large sections of rock?" Yael guided her horse around children playing in the street.

78

"Maybe, but what they're doing is building a double wall and filling it with the broken pieces. After we visit the market, we can return the long way so you can see the work going on."

"If it doesn't take too long. We need to be home before the sun's high. Don't you have a lot of packing to do?"

"Not really. Em and I rolled my cook pots in blankets and goatskins weeks ago. I have some clothes and perfumes, but they won't take long. Abba gave me two beautiful leather bags to carry them. One's already full."

Yael thought of the small goatskin bag her mother had handed her at the last minute. Her two robes didn't even fill it.

Sensing the direction of her thoughts, Eden asked, "Do you have something to wear to my wedding?"

"No."

"I'll lend you a robe I haven't packed yet."

"Thank you."

Eden looked at the sparse crowd in the open market. "Em said she needs olive oil. I know a good merchant to buy it from."

"I need to go see the family selling fruit. I'll be back shortly."

The young women slid off their horses and headed in opposite directions. Finding a fruit vendor, Yael chose and paid for a plump melon. "How are the grapes doing this year?"

"We didn't get as much of the latter rains as we wanted, but the good Lord sent a few showers after we'd given up expecting any, so the grapes are doing fair. Not as plump as they could be, but still a good crop," the old man reported.

"Excellent. I'm looking forward to the grape harvest," Yael answered.

After Yael rejoined Eden, they led their Arabians through the crowded market, pausing to bargain for the items Abigail and Elizabeth requested. Yael inhaled the fishy scent of the Jerusalem market. "You might miss the fresh fish in Rabbah. Their market doesn't smell like Jerusalem's."

"I won't miss the odor, but I will miss the taste of fish with em's herbs."

"Do you know your mother's recipes? It will be hard to get them after you leave."

"I know most of them. I'd better think through the special holiday meals and make sure I remember how to make the dishes for *Pesach*."

The girls remounted, and each followed her own thoughts as they headed for Eden's home by the circuitous route near the wall.

"What are you looking at?" Eden asked as they approached the Mishneh Gate. She followed Yael's gaze to a group of men with their robes girded so they could work unhampered. "Admiring all the hairy legs?" she asked, wrinkling her nose.

"I..." Yael broke off as she realized how uncouth she must seem to the cosmopolitan priest's daughter. "That man looks like David, my betrothed. I've seen David working the vineyard hundreds of times, but he wouldn't be here. He'd be home ensuring the best grape harvest possible so I can come home..."

She shaded her eyes from the sun. "Wait! That *is* David, and some others from our town."

"Daviiid!" she yelled.

Immediately one of the figures straightened from his work and fixed his attention on the approaching riders. He
80

vaulted off the wall onto the path and ran to them. "Yael, Yael, is that really you?"

He swung her off the horse as all the Gibeonites working on the wall called out greetings. "Your em's been so worried, but here you are riding a fine horse down a street in Jerusalem. Why are you here?"

"I could ask you the same thing," Yael said sharply. "Why aren't you home taking care of the vineyard?"

"All the work's caught up, matok. Raisa and I moved more transplants to the portion of vineyard your abba gave us last year. I managed to build a bit of a stone wall too. It's not high, but it's a start."

"What about the pruning?"

"Your abba and Gili are working from dawn to dark. Jarah and her boys have been carrying water and serving meals.

"We agonized over whether I should come work on Jerusalem's walls or not, but this is such an important project. A group of men came under Melatiah's leadership, and instead of your relatives leaving the vineyard, I came."

Reassured about their livelihood, Yael relaxed. "It *is* good to see you," Drinking in the sight of his familiar features, she said, "You look thirsty. Do you have something to drink while we catch up? How is my family? Is Ebin much bigger?"

David laughed and held up a hand to stem the flood of questions. "My water skin's in the shade. Let's go sit. Your family is well. Ebin grows every day."

"Yael, it's almost noon," Eden reminded her.

"Oh, Eden, I'm so sorry. I didn't expect to find my betrothed here. I forgot everything else." Yael blushed at her poor manners.

"Eden, this is David." Yael turned her attention back to David. "Eden is the daughter of Priest Meshullam. She's the reason I'm here and not in Rabbah. She's marrying Tobiah's son Johanan, the one I rode with when I left home."

Yael paused, and a dry sob escaped. "Being here has made me more homesick, and now seeing you, but having to leave again."

"When do you leave?" David asked gently.

"In three days. Will I be able to see you again?" Yael looked at him hopefully.

"Where are you staying?"

"Eliashib, the high priest's."

"I'll come see you."

"The wedding's tomorrow. Give us the next day to recover and come the day after."

"I'll come as soon as the sun gets hot, but for now I have to get back to work." The couple rose, and he cupped his big work-worn hands so she could mount the bay.

"I miss you so much, David."

"I miss you too. We're halfway through this separation. I'm glad to know they're treating you well. Go with God."

21

An insistent knock roused Johanan from his marriage bed. Reluctantly he left the feel of his new wife's silky skin and flowery aroma. *Who would bother a groom on his second night with a new bride?*

Tobiah's voice hissed. "Come out here, son. This is important."

Pulling a tunic over his head, Johanan groused, "More important than my lovely bride?" He emerged into the dimly lit hall, guessing it was the end of the second watch.

"We leave at dawn."

"What? Wait! We were to spend one more night. I'm not going to make Eden spend tonight packing. It's bad enough we're not getting our wedding week."

"You'll get it when you reach Rabbah."

Johanan struggled to focus his sleep-fogged brain. "Aren't you coming to Rabbah with us?"

"No, I need to see Sanballat in Samaria immediately. You can take the servants and go on to Rabbah without me. I'll be a few more days."

Johanan sighed. "What happened this time?"

"Nothing for a new husband to bother himself about. I'll tell the servants to prepare Eden's bundles. Her father sent them over today."

"Are we in danger?"

"Of course not, boy. It's a business matter."

Business the night after my wedding? "Very well, father. Alert the servants. Eden and I will be ready."

⌘⌘

Silent tears tracked down Yael's face as she stuffed Noa's belongings into a leather bag and her own into her ugly goatskin sack. She took them to the sleepy servant who stacked them with the other bundles to lash onto the donkeys in a few hours.

Lying down again next to Noa, she scrambled for ideas about how to see David. She needed more news from home. She fell into an exhausted sleep only to be roused by an irate Tobiah for oversleeping. Quickly she found Noa's sandals, and they both gulped down some cold water before joining the confusion of nearly a dozen animals in the courtyard. *What must Eliashib's household think of us?*

Johanan emerged with Eden. He settled her onto her blanketed gray filly while the groom boosted Noa onto her mount.

Yael felt panicked. David wasn't coming until later. Seeing one of the servant girls bring skins of water, she approached her. "Please. My betrothed was supposed to visit me here today. Could you tell him our group left early? I don't know why, but it was sudden. Could you please tell him? His name is David of Gibeon. He's been working on the wall."

Tobiah rushed out of the house and leaped onto his mount. With an impatient wave of his arm, he signaled the cavalcade to start moving. Yael looked pleadingly at the young servant.

The girl watched Tobiah with thinly veiled animosity. "Your master's not worth a lick of salt, but I suppose that isn't your fault. I'll tell your man. Don't worry."

Relief flooded Yael as she hurried to her bay and exited the gate before the baggage animals. Catching up to Noa, she admired the city as best she could in the meager light.

Their entourage swept through the streets, out the east gate with barely a wave to Shecaniah, and picked up the pace as Tobiah rushed down the incline.

When the sun had fully risen and Tobiah showed no signs of slowing, Johanan said, "Yael, watch over Eden as well as Noa. I need to get my father to slow down." He whispered to his chestnut who lunged forward in response.

"These horses are built for speed," Yael said.

"Yes, but I'm not," Eden answered.

As Yael studied Eden more closely, she realized the bride was in pain and dropped back beside her.

"Too much jostling too close to my wedding night," Eden explained.

Yael ran the words through her mind until they made sense and grimaced in sympathy. "Did you pack any cushions in the luggage?"

"My em did, but I don't know which bundle it ended up in. We might have to unroll all of them to find it. And Tobiah's in too much of a hurry. Do you know why?"

"I have no idea." Yael sighed. "David was going to come see me today."

"I'm so sorry. This is crazy. Is Tobiah always like this?"

"Thankfully I haven't spent much time around him, but yes, based on what I've seen, he's always like this."

Johanan circled back. "We can slow down. My father will take a few servants and go to Samaria. We'll branch off to Jericho today. Maybe we'll even spend tomorrow there," he added, after studying Eden's white face.

"As soon as we stop for a break, we need to poke around in the luggage and see if we can locate a cushion," Yael said.

"Good idea," Johanan agreed. "Let's get down this mountain and find a place to stop."

Since Jericho wasn't a hard day's ride, the group chose a leisurely pace. Eden insisted on a long lunch, so they didn't arrive at the ancient city until late afternoon.

Yael waited on Eden, trying to make her comfortable at the best inn Jericho offered. Eden was so exhausted she could barely string together an intelligible request. The innkeeper sent water, so Yael gently wiped off the grime of the road, shook dust out of a fresh robe, and arranged a thick stack of blankets for Eden's bed.

Then Yael put Noa to bed and retreated to the roof for the cool night air, her thoughts in a tangle.

The night sky made her feel small, insignificant. *Oh, David, did the girl give you my message? I wanted to see you again, listen to your deep voice tell me all I've missed at home. Those few moments we talked weren't enough. And why aren't you doing everything possible to ensure a good harvest? Our future depends on it.*

She turned at the sound of footsteps on the stone stairs. Johanan headed for her. Hastily she wiped her eyes and covered half her face with her headscarf. *At least this thing will hide the tears even if it's suffocating.*

86

Johanan leaned his elbows on the wall and looked out at the Judean desert surrounding the oasis of Jericho. "How's she doing?"

"It would be good to rest at least two days. She's complaining about being sore."

Johanan swore under his breath. "I can't believe my father did this to us."

"Why did we leave so suddenly?"

"My father wasn't thrilled to see the wall being rebuilt, but he figured the Jews can do whatever they want if he could make some gold. He went to the Tirshatha and tried to sell him limestone—at exorbitant prices, I'm sure. When the man wouldn't deal with him, he tried to talk Eliashib into helping him get the business, but the high priest said he has no influence with the new governor. My father became enraged. Thence our hasty departure."

"I can understand his desire to sell them Ammonite limestone. It's good trade for our country, and he'd receive a commission, but why get so upset when his proposition was rejected? Looked to me like they had enough rock to rebuild to a formidable height. And why the day after my wedding?" Johanan groaned.

Yael listened in sympathetic silence, unsure of what to say.

Johanan sighed and looked at her more closely. "Enough about me. What's wrong? Are you more homesick after this trip?"

My red-rimmed eyes gave me away. "I was supposed to see my betrothed today."

Johanan smacked his forehead. "That's right! Eden told me you saw him working on the wall with others from your hometown. I'm sorry, Yael. I guess you know by now my father thinks only of himself."

"That was my first impression of him," Yael said bitterly.

"Yes, you know that better than most.

"Maybe I can convince him to give your family more time to pay for the vineyard. They'll have the thirteen coins for you by the end of harvest, won't they?"

"They should. I have no idea how they can come up with the other forty so quickly. No one in Gibeon has that kind of money. My mother weaves gorgeous Persian rugs, but they're time consuming. She had just started one."

"I won't let your family end up homeless, Yael."

"Thank you."

As dusk fell, Johanan pushed away from the ledge. "I'm going to retire. Sleep in tomorrow if you like."

"See you in the morning." Since no one was around, Yael freed her face from the veil and studied the stars and their constellations, comforted by Johanan's promise. *Adonai knows the names of all these stars. Surely He's watching out for this daughter of Yehud too.*

22

Yael slept until the sun was well over the horizon. She hurried to find Noa since the little girl's mat was empty. Noa and Johanan were munching on figs and pomegranates in the main room of the inn.

"You look refreshed this morning," Johanan said.

"It was good to make up some sleep," Yael agreed. "How's Eden?"

"Still sleeping. When she wakes up, I'll see if she'd like to walk to the market. Maybe some of the goods we need are less expensive than those in Rabbah. Sit down, have something to eat."

A servant filled her cup with wine, and Noa ran out to a courtyard to play with the innkeeper's children under the watchful eyes of Johanan's groom. "This is much better than yesterday," Yael said.

"Every day away from my father is better," Johanan answered. "I wonder what trouble he's stirring up today. I know he went to Samaria to speak with Sanballat."

Johanan spit out pomegranate seeds. "Sanballat won't be happy to hear about Jerusalem's new walls either."

"Why do they care?"

"Jerusalem's weakness made them feel powerful. They could enter and exit the city as they wished since most of the gates were missing. No one bothered to fix the gates because the breaches in the wall would allow entrance anyway."

"Can't your father get into Jerusalem any time he wants through your grandfather's gate?"

"Yes, probably, unless all the gates are shut by the Tirshatha's orders. Men like my father and the governor of Samaria feel threatened when anyone else improves his lot. They think it diminishes them somehow."

"Oh."

"Jerusalem will be more secure against marauders once the walls are raised. Your betrothed is doing important work." Johanan paused. "Why isn't he preparing for the grape harvest though? Your family's future hangs on this one harvest."

A frisson of anxiety rippled through Yael. "He said my father and uncle have everything under control. Raisa, my younger sister, has been doing a lot more work. My mother's best friend has four boys, and they're hauling water and doing other tasks. David will return before harvest."

"Oh, no!" she moaned. "I just realized harvest will probably take longer since so many villagers are working on the wall. Usually the entire village joins in until it's done."

"There will be a ready market for the new wine in Jerusalem," Johanan comforted her.

"I hadn't thought of that. I suppose you're right. But if abba sells it all as new wine, he won't be able to put aside jars to age. He tries to save at least a dozen since they bring more shekels."

90

"That's wise."

"He was selling aged wine when your father came to our home. That money's always stretched through the end of the winter and into the beginning of planting season. What a mess! Maybe they should pay for the vineyard first, and redeem me when they can. Em's rug will bring in enough shekels."

"I'm sorry I've brought it up again and worried you."

"It's never far from my thoughts..." Yael's voice trailed off. "But I need to concentrate on today and what I can control, little though it may be. Would you like me to go check on Eden?"

"I'd appreciate that. I won't go any farther than the stables."

The wedding group lingered two days in Jericho before fording the trickling Jordan and camping one evening in the open on the way to Rabbah.

23

S halom, my new daughter," Abigail greeted them. "Congratulations, son. Come here, Noa, and give your em a hug. I missed you. I want to hear all the details of the wedding. Where's your father?"

"I'll explain while the ladies go in and wash before dinner." Johanan lifted Eden from her mount while a servant assisted Yael. Noa vaulted off her horse.

"The nomad's blood runs strong in *your* veins," Abigail said as Noa hugged her in passing. "Cook will start serving as soon as you're ready."

Taking his mother's arm, Johanan said, "Father's gone to Samaria to see Sanballat."

"Sanballat! That man's nothing but trouble. Do you know why he went?"

"There's a new Tirshatha in Jerusalem, and he has the people rebuilding the walls. Father's upset about it."

"New walls? That will be wonderful. The Jews will be much safer." Abigail paused. "Right after Rabbi Ezra came, one of his daughters was attacked in the city. Caused such a stir even I heard of it. She outwitted her attackers on the wall, and falling stone crushed one of them. I wish I'd met her, but I already lived here. You must have been about six at the time, Johanan. Your grandmother came when your brother Lot was born and told me all the news."

"So why's your father against walls?" Abigail asked.

"The immediate reason is they won't buy Ammonite limestone through him."

"Sounds like your father." Abigail sighed. "I'm sure he'll be back for your wedding celebration in ten days. Will you stay here until then or go check on the herds?"

"Father was supposed to check on them so I could spend time with my bride. Even though we traveled slowly for her sake, she had some difficulty. I'll stay here with her and introduce her to the city. We need to purchase wares for my tent so she'll be comfortable when we travel with the herds."

"I think that's a good decision. I'm sure your brother and the servants are managing well."

"Eden's not the only one who had a hard trip. I'm not sure it was a good idea for Yael."

"Why?" Abigail asked.

"She helped Eden tremendously." Johanan stopped walking. "But Yael found her betrothed working on the wall. Since father made us leave early, she didn't get to talk with him much."

Johanan started walking again, his jaw set. "Yael's betrothed should have been focusing on making her family's grape harvest successful."

"Yael's a wonderful girl, a hard worker. She deserves the best. If she's unable to return…" Abigail looked at Johanan hopefully.

"They'll have the money to redeem her, but her family may lose the vineyard. I need to persuade father to give them more time to buy it. Vineyard keepers don't make forty silver pieces in a year, above and beyond what they need to live."

"Let's hope he returns in a good mood."

Johanan patted his mother's arm. "From your lips to God's ears."

24

Tobiah arrived in the courtyard in a cloud of summer dust. Yael choked on his presence as much as the dust, but stayed so the three children could greet their father. He barely acknowledged them.

Abigail floated down the stairs in a sky-blue gown with a silver goblet of wine. He eyed her appreciatively.

"I knew you'd return before the wedding dinner," she said.

"We'll have more guests to celebrate with," Tobiah announced. "I invited Sanballat. He's attending to a few matters, so will arrive tomorrow."

Abigail stiffened slightly. "I'm pleased he can join us. How many will he bring?"

"At least twenty." Tobiah didn't see the lines of stress his pronouncement added to his wife's face.

When he turned to pick up Noa, Abigail beckoned Yael and whispered, "Go to the butcher before he closes for the evening, and bring home enough to feed thirty more. Sanballat always travels with a retinue."

Glad for the chance to escape, Yael mounted the gray nag and headed for the market. Chagrined, she examined the sparse end-of-day selection. "This porker would feed thirty hungry men," the muscular butcher recommended.

Abigail wouldn't want to spend good silver for goat meat. The family owned plenty of goats. Yael agreed the pig was the best option, but could she bring herself to buy pork?

God forgive me. She arranged for its delivery and hurried back ahead of the slave who dealt with the carcass and attendant cloud of flies.

Cook deftly rubbed the meat with herbs and put it on a spit to roast slowly until the following evening. "Gonna be a long night," she sighed.

"Wake me for the third watch. I'll make sure nothing burns," Yael promised. "You can get a few hours uninterrupted sleep."

Cook looked at her in surprise. "A blessing—that's what you are. I'm going to miss you when you're gone." She stirred the mixture in one of the clay pots. "I know I can trust you to watch the food. There's not many I can say that about."

A warm glow suffused Yael, though she knew she'd be tired as she watched children and served at the wedding feast the next day.

⌘⌘

At the wedding celebration, Yael served wine as the guests danced in separate groups of men and women. Dinner would be served, and then more dancing, where the men and women would dance with each other.

The revelers were becoming more and more rowdy as they drank more aged wine. It was about time they put something else in their stomachs.

Yael attempted to keep distance between herself and the increasingly drunk Arabs who came with an uninvited Bedouin named Geshem. Sanballat had invited him. The nerve of some people! Tobiah deserved a friend like Sanballat, but Abigail didn't need him complicating plans at her son's wedding feast.

Sanballat and Tobiah belonged together like a mortar and pestle. Unfortunately, the duo was likely to crush someone. *Adonai, please protect Abigail.*

Lost in her musings, Yael wasn't quick enough to escape one Arab's groping hands. Flustered, she nearly dropped the jug of wine. "You're familiar with nomad hospitality, pretty one?" he leered.

Yael's stomach clenched. He wanted her to share his pallet tonight. Common practice except in Yehud.

Pretending she hadn't heard, she retreated to the kitchen. Leaning against a wall, she sucked in deep breaths, staving off panic and tears. *Adonai, deliver me!*

She hadn't married David because she hadn't yet reached womanhood in Yehud. Her monthly flow began after she'd arrived in Rabbah. Would she now lose her virginity, or even become with child?

"What's wrong, girl?" Cook asked.

"A man out there, one of the Arabs... He wants..." Yael couldn't continue.

"Say no more," Cook said. "Keep serving him wine. Smile like you're interested in a tryst, but keep his goblet full from this pitcher. It's stronger, for the bride and groom. He'll pass out before he can lay a hand on you."

"Thank you! Thank you." Yael nearly wept.

"Here, refill Johanan's and his wife's and then sashay over to the lout who's bothering you. Can you handle a pitcher in each hand? They don't have to be full. It will be more convincing if you refill goblets with the regular wine all along your way to his couch. That's a good girl. It will be all right." She handed Yael both pitchers and gave her a gentle push toward the revelers.

"Like sending an innocent kid out among lions," she muttered as she turned back to the hearth.

Trying to play her part, Yael swayed her hips as she sauntered away from pouring the bushy-bearded Arab's third cup of strong wine. He was disgusting, and she felt ridiculous.

The last time she'd tried to entice a man with her walk she was ten, in the vineyard, walking away from David with a dipper of water she'd brought him. It worked too. Her first true smile of the night tipped her lips.

Johanan caught her grin. "It's good to see you looking happy. You looked like you wanted to stomp on some toes earlier tonight. Come dance with the groom." He held out his arms.

Yael lowered her eyes, set the wine pitchers on a small serving table, and held Johanan's hands like the other women held their partners. "I've never done this before, so your toes are at a definite disadvantage."

"Seems like you've experienced a lot of firsts with me." The look in his eyes made Yael's stomach flip.

He's a bit drunk, and is thinking of Eden. That's all. But his arms pulled her closer. He was light on his feet, so by simply following, Yael matched the dance's steps with ease. His scent tickled her senses. *If she hadn't loved David since she was a girl...*

The dance ended with a flourish of drums, and Yael stepped away. "I should get back to serving."

98

"And I to my bride." But the gleam in his eye grew stronger.

On her next circuit through the room, the Arab looked heavy eyed. She deftly filled his cup and tipped the rest of the other pitcher into Geshem's goblet. Then she retreated to the kitchen to refill. She noticed Johanan and Eden had retired for the evening.

"Your plan's working," she informed Cook.

"Good, but we're out of the strong drink."

"I think it will be fine. The bride and groom retired to their chamber, and Tobiah's past the point of noticing."

Cook lowered her voice. "Is he making a fool of himself?"

"Not yet, but there's still time."

"Have something to eat before you go back with the wine." Cook set a portion of lamb on the wooden table.

"Thank you. I am hungry."

"Of course you are. All these good smells, and you haven't eaten a bite yet. One reason I like cooking is I never go hungry." Cook patted her ample mid-section. "I often don't sit to eat, but a taste here and there to make sure it's properly seasoned goes a long way."

"Your lamb is delicious."

"It's the seasonings and slow roasting. My mother taught me how."

"Could you show me? This is a dish I could make at home."

"Next time I prepare it you can be my assistant."

Yael swallowed her last morsel of savory meat and rose. "I need to get back out there. The women were all leaving. How long will the men stay?"

"Sometimes they drink until morning." Cook handed her a full carafe. "Abigail will let us sleep tomorrow if that happens."

When Yael reentered the courtyard, only a few candles remained lit. The men's voices were hushed. She refilled cups with watered-down wine, catching the phrases "Jerusalem's walls" and "curse the new Tirshatha."

Yael stood quietly in the shadows watching for emptying goblets. She pinched herself to keep awake and studied the brilliant stars.

"Death to the Jews!" Geshem shouted.

Yael jumped and edged closer.

"How many soldiers do you have ready to fight?" Geshem asked Sanballat.

"Five hundred, and I could raise another five hundred within the week."

"That will be plenty with my two bands of warriors."

"The Jews won't stand a chance. You can attack from two sides of the city," Tobiah said. "I can show you the best way to approach from the east."

Yael felt a flutter of movement behind her. A hand clamped on her arm and pulled her back up the hall to the kitchen. She tried to move with as little noise as possible so the plotters wouldn't remember her presence. In the kitchen's flickering firelight, she turned to face Abigail.

"He's going to lead them to my father's gate. My father will be one of the first to be..." Tears glistened in Abigail's eyes.

Yael felt like cold water had been thrown on her, invigorating her body and mind. "We'll warn them. If it's not a sneak attack, it will fail. Sanballat and Geshem don't have enough soldiers, and Jerusalem's on a mountain. If the Jews are watching for them, they can fight their enemies off. There are plenty of men in the city."

Abigail considered. "You may be right. How can we get a message to them?"

Yael mulled it over. "Through Dael. It will look normal if he takes a caravan or sends his servants to trade."

"Good idea. Go get some sleep. We'll go to the souk as soon as it opens in a few hours. I'll get one of the other servants to keep plying the men with wine."

Yael stumbled off to her pallet in the children's room. She thought she'd never fall asleep, but her racing heart slowed, and their even breathing lulled her to sleep.

25

Abigail quietly woke Yael after the sun rose. They slipped out of the room, leaving the children to sleep off the excitement of the previous day. If Abigail's red eyes were any indication, she hadn't slept at all.

The courtyard was a shambles, goblets and bits of food strewn amidst sticky spots on the stone. But there were no drunks sleeping in the corners. Abigail pressed her eyes shut. "We'll have to clean this up when we return." Exhaustion laced her pronouncement.

Yael urged her to sit on a bench as they waited for two mounts. "We'll buy some herbs and spices for Cook. She ran out preparing the meat for Johanan's feast," Abigail said. The purchase would place them in proximity to Dael's shop.

After mounting two bays, they trotted to the market at a fast clip. Abigail made her purchases, and Yael caught the merchant trying to short-change them. Abigail had caught countless such "mistakes." Even in the throes of childbirth, she had kept her wits. Now her distress showed plainly.

There were no shoppers in Dael's store at this early hour. A guard and a clerk greeted them.

"Is Dael here?" Abigail inquired.

"Right here, my esteemed customer," Dael replied, emerging from the storeroom.

"We need to speak privately," Abigail said in a low voice. Dael dispatched the clerk on an errand and retreated to the back corner of the store so the guard posted at the front could not hear their conversation. He began flipping through the expensive rugs.

"How can I be of assistance?"

"At my son's feast, some of the late-goers were plotting against our people," Abigail explained.

"No doubt that riff-raff with Sanballat."

"Yes, the Arabs and Sanballat and ..." Abigail faltered.

When her mistress seemed unable to continue, Yael added, "Tobiah offered to show them a way into the city from the east."

Dael looked concerned. "Where your father mans his gate."

Abigail's eyes welled with tears.

Dael closed his eyes and inhaled before turning his attention back to Abigail. "Now, my dear, He who watches over Israel will neither slumber nor sleep. He allowed you to hear their plot, and we'll warn our people. The Jews have already built the walls to half their height. Don't be afraid.

"I have a small caravan that just passed through Jerusalem. One box of spice wasn't ready, so I'll send a few men to fetch it. They can take a message to your father, Abigail. All will be well."

"How soon can they leave?" Abigail asked.

"Before the sun is high."

"Surely they'll arrive well before Sanballat can muster his army," Yael said.

"Yes," Dael said. "The Jews will have plenty of warning. What else did you hear that I can include in the message?"

"Sanballat has access to five hundred men immediately and five hundred more by the week's end. Geshem said he has two bands of warriors. I don't know how many that would be," Yael said.

"Probably about sixty," Dael mused. "You ladies return home. Don't worry about anything. My men should arrive in Jerusalem in two days. I'll tell them to go straight to Shecaniah at the east gate with a message about a plot by a thousand Samaritans and Arabs against the city. Without the element of surprise, our enemies won't succeed. Archers alone can defend the city since it's on high ground.

"If you'll excuse me, I have arrangements to make. Yael, make sure your mistress rests as soon as she reaches home. Go with God." He ushered them out the front door and boosted them onto their horses.

Abigail could hardly stay on her Arabian she was so tired. After dismounting, Yael supported her as they crossed the courtyard. *Like she supported me when I first arrived at this house, scared and alone. Now we've come full circle, our lives bound together.*

Abigail smiled faintly when she saw one servant girl scrubbing the courtyard under Cook's supervision. While Abigail sat on a stone bench, Yael washed her mistress' feet. She accompanied her to the bedchamber and waited until Abigail's breathing indicated she'd drifted to sleep.

Yael returned to the courtyard and picked up refuse with Noa and Hymie. They finished before the summer sun melted the scraps to the stones. The groom continued eliminating the worst of the stains. The sun would bleach the rest.

Yael and Cook fed the children figs and flat bread. After settling the little ones for a nap, Yael lay down nearby. When she woke, the air felt cooler.

She took the children out to play in the courtyard. As she watched them, one of Dael's servants was admitted through the gate.

He approached the bench where she sat under a fig tree. "My master has a message for you to relay to your mistress. He's sent a heavily armed caravan to Jerusalem. They'll request lodging at her father's home. He says to thank her for the invitation."

Puzzled, Yael went to find Abigail. "Dael sent a message to you through me. An armed caravan left for Jerusalem this morning. They plan to ask your father to stay with him."

"Did he say anything else?"

"Yes, but it didn't make sense to me. He said to thank you for the lodging invitation."

The worry on Abigail's face changed to relief. "Dael's telling me these extra men will stay with my father and be ready to fight at the east gate. Bless him! And he left the message with you, so Tobiah won't hear about it from one of the other servants."

"He's a good man."

"Yes, and a good Jew."

Yael fidgeted with a loose thread on her robe. "You and Dael both love our people. How did you end up in Rabbah?"

"His father didn't have enough property for all his sons, so Dael took a business opportunity here.

"As for me, I begged my father to let me marry Tobiah. Tobiah has always visited Jerusalem. He used to bring me little gifts, things we couldn't get in Jerusalem. I was tired of being a poor girl in a poor backwater of a city. I thought I'd have a better life here."

"Your home is nicer than any of the ones in my village. Is it better than where you grew up?"

"Definitely, but remember we live with the herds most of the time. And I've learned living in a finer house doesn't mean having a better life." Her mistress fell silent, and Yael thought the discussion had ended, but Abigail added, "Do you think you're marrying into a better life?"

"No. I've loved David since I was a girl of about seven. He's worked in the vineyard ever since I can remember. His family's poorer than mine because David's father was injured in an attack before I was born. They have a little house I'd move into. We were starting some new vines at the uncultivated edges of the vineyard, but those vines would belong to your husband's sister too.

"Does she really want payment for the vineyard? It seems strange that she'd ask after all this time."

"I don't know. I haven't seen Judith for years, since before she married. She lives in Susa. Is married to an extremely wealthy merchant named Ctesias."

"Then why would she care about fifty silver pieces?"

"It doesn't seem like she would. All this started when Tobiah's father died, and Tobiah went through his old records."

"Yes, he showed us the marriage agreement. The vineyard was supposed to revert to her in the case of a divorce. It just seems odd she'd ask now."

"People tend to wrap things up when there's a death in the family. It gives a sense of closure, finished business. I don't know if it's Judith who wants the closure, or my husband."

26

Jarah paused as the temple mount appeared, crowning Jerusalem. She never tired of the view, and now walls protected the temple and the citizens of Jerusalem. Her husband was up there laboring with other men from Gibeon. This wall had been her dream since she first set foot in the city fourteen years earlier.

Her three oldest boys eyed her with amusement when she started singing off-key. She ignored them as she praised her Creator for gifting her with four healthy boys. She had left Gedalya, the youngest, with a neighbor, but the rest were old enough to remove rubbish.

When David returned to Gibeon to catch up with the vineyard's work before harvest, he had relayed Nehemiah's request for workers to haul away refuse.

When Naama assured her the harvest was two or three weeks away, Jarah decided to join her husband in Jerusalem and contribute to the effort on the wall. *Hope Oren will be happy I've come with the boys. I'll know soon enough.*

David said the Gibeonites were working near the Old Gate, so Jarah steered her boys in that direction. When the boys saw their fellow townsmen, they broke into a run. Jarah took the donkey's reins from Jabin and followed, watching for Oren's reaction. He seemed pleased to see his sons and looked past them for her. Straightening his robe, he walked to meet her, taking the donkey.

"This is a surprise."

"David said hands were needed to clear rubbish," Jarah explained.

Oren beckoned his sons and started toward the home they'd bought for a Jerusalem residence. For several months a year, they stayed in this house while he fulfilled his duties as a Levite.

"The boys can remove refuse, and you can cook for us. Our house is bursting at the seams with Gibeonites who have no family to live with while they're building the wall."

When Jarah began to protest, Oren held up his hand. "You are not going to sully and roughen your hands on these walls. I know you've prayed for walls since you first saw this city, but Adonai has other work for your hands. Do I need to remind you of all the cloth needed for the temple? You need to protect your hands for weaving. And no, before you suggest it, covering them with rags won't be enough."

Jarah bowed her head.

"I know you're bursting to help rebuild. Feeding us will be no small feat and will free one of us men to work longer. Not to mention you're a much better cook. I've never eaten so much burnt stew. I'm glad you're here, Jarah."

He tipped her head up so he could look her in the eye. "Your contribution is barreling down the road behind us."

Jarah turned to look at the three sturdy boys, and her heart rose. "God is good."

108

"That he is, matok. But we seem to be missing one."

"I left Gedalya with Tova. At four, he would be in the way more than he would help."

"I agree. Praise Adonai for a wife of understanding." As they reached their two-story Jerusalem home, Oren removed the packs from the donkey. "There's feed in our stable, Jabin. Care for our beast while I get your mother settled. Then we'll return to the wall until sunset.

"Menachem, look who's come to relieve you of your cooking duties," Oren boomed as they entered the house.

"Shalom, Jarah. How is my Tova?"

"Shalom. She and the children are well. I added to her burdens by leaving Gedalya with them."

"He's a good boy. I'm sure he'll fetch wood and water and earn his keep."

"I told him he must. At most we can stay two weeks. Ariel and Naama will need help with the harvest."

"There may not be many harvesters this year," Menachem noted.

"Then we'll have to work extra hard. They need a good harvest to redeem Yael and pay for the vineyard."

"Forty pieces of silver is a lot for one harvest," Menachem said.

At the open front door, a Jew on horseback maneuvered through the children, shouting for Oren. All three adults went back outside. "The Tirshatha's calling a meeting in front of the temple. Get there as fast as you can. The Samaritans are planning to attack. Bring your weapons."

He whirled away before anyone could ask questions.

Oren hugged Jarah. "We still need you to prepare our evening meal. I'll take Jabin with me in case I need to send word to you." He looked at the younger boys. "Hoshea and Doran, stay inside with your mother."

"I think I'm making a mess of dinner, Jarah. I'm sorry I can't stay to explain what I've done to the bread," Menachem said as he strapped on a sword.

"I'll sort it out," Jarah said, turning to the hearth as the men set off at a run. She sampled the stew, which was passable, added a pinch of herbs, and then looked at the sticky mass of dough.

"Ay, these men do need my help." She added barley flour and kneaded until it was the right consistency. *But did I endanger my boys by bringing them here? Adonai, please deliver us.*

27

When Nehemiah stood on the steps outside the temple, every man, woman, and child quieted. "Brothers, our enemies the Samaritans, Arabians, and Ammonites are planning to attack us to stop our work on the wall. You need to gather your weapons and stand watch where you've been working.

"We've received reports from Jews who live near them. One came late yesterday, five more today. A few were sent from prominent citizens in Rabbah and Samaria.

"Benjamin and I will come around and set watchmen for tonight. Most of you need to sleep at the wall so we'll be ready. Send a few of your men back to your houses to sleep well so they can watch tomorrow.

"No lights shining in our city tonight. The watchmen need to keep their night vision, and it will make us less of a target."

"What if our tents are outside the city?" a thin, nervous-looking man asked.

"If you've been camping outside the city walls, bring your families and possessions inside. Eliashib, will you pray for us?"

The elderly priest shuffled forward, lifted his hands. "God of heaven and earth, we are doing your work, repairing the walls. Our enemies are coming against us once again. Deliver your people."

"Amen," the crowd echoed, immediately scattering to their tasks.

Nehemiah and Benjamin conferred in the court of Gentiles. "I don't know anything about warfare," Benjamin said, rubbing his ear.

Nehemiah realized it wasn't the time to admit he didn't either. "Our Lord, who is great and terrible, is with us. Right now, we need to organize the men. You have plenty of experience with managing men. For the most part, they're already in place.

"Size up the men and divide them into two groups. Pay careful attention to their eyesight. We need men with sharp eyesight on each watch. Put one group on the wall to guard it. Let the other rest behind it, close enough to provide reinforcements during an attack. Make sure there are archers in each group. Have them switch places every twelve hours.

"We have a lot of ground to cover, so we need to split up and move quickly. If you find men with soldiering experience, send them back to my house so we can formulate a plan to defend our city. May God's favor deliver us."

⌘⌘

Oren and Jabin returned within the hour. "Melatiah sent me back for the night, but most of the others will have to guard the wall. We'll bring them dinner when it's ready. It smells heavenly." He sniffed appreciatively.

"Just needed a few more herbs. It's ready," Jarah answered. "Is the enemy within range of the city?"

"No one's seen an army approaching. Our informers found out about the attack when it was in the planning and mobilizing phase."

"Are they reliable?"

"Six sources' stories match up. Jews who live in Rabbah and Samaria," Oren said. "Jabin, ask the neighbors if you can borrow their cart to tote this kettle of stew."

"Yes, Abba." The boy scampered off.

"Now I can enjoy my wife," Oren said, gathering Jarah in his arms and inhaling her scent.

"Get on with you! It was a hot, dusty journey and now I'm working over a hot fire."

"Doesn't matter. I've been around a bunch of sweaty men for over a moon. You smell like lavender."

Jarah's eyes lit up. "I've missed you too."

Jabin returned with the cart, the neighbor's donkey already harnessed to the traces. "The neighbors just got back from helping some families move their tents from outside the city. He said to take his donkey too."

"The men will be happy to get their dinner faster," Oren agreed. "Come, boys."

Jarah placed the unleavened bread in a basket. "More's coming. Jabin, you stay here until it's done. Then you can catch up."

Jabin looked disappointed, but a look from his father elicited a polite, "Yes, em."

With Jabin's help, Jarah packed olives, grapes and figs into two large baskets. "Be careful," Jarah told him. "The streets are much busier than in Gibeon." Jabin set off at a trot.

When Jabin reached the Gibeonites, the men were ignoring the dinner his father and brothers had delivered. On high alert, they studied the terrain sloping down from Jerusalem.

"I see a slight movement and some dust," one said.

"I see it too, but I don't think it's an army," Melatiah answered, squinting.

Jabin looked in the direction they pointed. "It's a herd of sheep or goats."

"You can see it clearly?" Oren asked.

"I see animals and two shepherds."

"He has sharp eyes, Oren," the first man said as all the men on the wall focused on the boy.

Embarrassed, Jabin mumbled, "It's nothing. You should ask Hoshea what he sees out there. He'll know whether they're sheep or goats."

Oren called the two boys playing behind the wall, "Hoshea, Doran, come up here."

"Yes, Abba," the youngsters answered as they scaled the rough wall.

"Do you see the herd?"

The boys nodded.

"Are they sheep or goats?" Oren asked.

"Goats," nine-year-old Hoshea answered without hesitation. The men squinted.

"All I see is green and brown," one admitted.

"Me too," said Menachem.

"There's an eagle above the herd," seven-year-old Doran said matter-of-factly.

His father looked at him in amazement. "You can see a bird that far away?"

"Not any bird." He shrugged. "Eagles are big."

"Jabin, can you see the eagle?" Oren asked.

114

"I can see a speck circling. I'm sure Doran's right. He wins every time we play the sight game, although Gedalaya's starting to get things right just as often."

Thunderstruck, Oren stared at his boys. Then a smile played on his lips. Melatiah thumped him on the back. "We found our look-outs, Oren. Can you spare them for a while?"

"Absolutely, though you'll have to keep them on task."

"We can do that. An adult will stay with them at all times, and they can take turns, for a shorter watch than one of us would take. I feel like I've found a honey tree or a vein of gold."

Oren clasped the boys' shoulders. "Their mother and I always knew they were precious." Turning to his sons, he said, "Boys, keep close watch. Soldiers are coming to attack us and destroy our work on the wall. If you see them, tell the others, and then come home where you'll be safe. You're not old enough to fight."

"We'll look after them, Oren," Melatiah promised. "Now which of you would like to be look-out first? This is going to be tough because the sun's going to be blinding as it sets."

"I see best at night," Jabin answered, "And I'm oldest so won't be as sleepy. Let Doran take this watch, then Hoshea until the end of the second watch. I'll take the third and most of the fourth watch. Then whoever's awake before dawn can be next."

"Good plan, Son. We'll stay with you all night. Oren, go spend time with your wife. Come back to collect Doran so he can sleep at home. The older boys can spend the night here."

"I'll bring you two some sleeping mats, and a goatskin for water. Remember what I said about coming home if we're attacked."

"We promise to obey, Abba."

Melatiah sent a few Gibeonites back with Oren, so they'd be rested the next day.

Jarah was patting her hair dry when Oren came through their front door. "I feel much better now that I've gotten rid of all that grime."

"I'm glad you got cleaned up, but a few of the men will be coming through the door soon. I got home faster in the donkey cart."

Jarah grabbed her head covering and adjusted it over her thick brown hair. "What about the boys?"

Oren explained.

"They do have keen eyesight," Jarah agreed. "They try to beat each other at some kind of game all the time. They've given up asking me to mediate their arguments about who wins. I can't see what they're talking about."

"Adonai's given them a skill that's coming in handy. Good thing you brought them." Oren sank onto a bench. "I'll go get Doran before we settle down to sleep. As soon as he wakes in the morning I'll take him back and bring the other boys home to sleep. I've told them all to come home when the attack begins."

"Do we know when the attack was planned for?"

"I haven't heard. Maybe I can find out more when I fetch Doran, but right now I intend to enjoy my dinner and my wife. It's been a long time since we've been alone with no children."

"But you said others will arrive soon."

"I claimed the small bed chamber upstairs for our family. No one will bother us later."

As they ate with the men, Jarah shared all the news from Gibeon. When she finished, the men asked questions about their wives and children. A few of the families had sent small bundles to their men. Jarah distributed them to those present and put the rest on a shelf near the hearth.

"I have a surprise for you too, matok," Oren said as the other men moved outside into the cooler air. "Hadassah's family returned with Tirshatha Nehemiah."

"Nooo!" Jarah squealed. "Do you know where I can find her?"

"They have a house near Nehemiah's because Benjamin's been planning the reconstruction of the wall."

"I can't wait to see her. I've never even met her children. To think she's made that dreadful journey two more times!"

"Well then, let's get going."

"I meant I'd find her in the morning."

Oren's lips twitched. "If you're sure you don't want her company more than mine..."

"Of course I don't. You'll be busy at the wall tomorrow. I'll look for her then," Jarah said, hands on her hips.

Oren captured her hands. "Let's retire for a few hours before I bring Doran home."

"Exactly what I was thinking."

28

Jarah was stirring lentils in a huge clay pot the next morning when Hadassah swept into the room with two young girls clutching her white linen robe.

"Jarah!" Hadassah cried as she hugged her.

"And who are these two beautiful girls?" Jarah asked, bending over to look them in the eyes. "Surely they're not both as shy as their mother."

Hadassah pointed to the eldest, "This is Rachel."

She nudged the younger. "And this little lady is Hallel.

"Girls, remember I've told you about my friend who walked across the desert with me on my first trip to Jerusalem?"

"Too far," Hallel said.

Jarah laughed loudly. "You are entirely right, Hallel. Did you walk the whole way?"

"No," Rachel said. "We rode with Abba or Uncle Nehemiah."

"We made it in just under two moons," Hadassah explained.

"I'm glad to hear you didn't have to walk it again," Jarah said. "Once is enough!"

118

"Agreed! I heard your boys are look-outs, so I guess I won't get to meet them today."

"Jabin's here sleeping since he watched most of the night."

"He was younger than Hallel last I saw him, and I met Hoshea as a baby," Hadassah said.

"We have two younger boys now. Doran's at the wall with Oren, but I left Gedalaya home with Tova."

"How is she?"

"She's good, busy with her three boys." Jarah's grin transformed her plain face.

"And Naama?"

Jarah's bright smile faded. "Now there's a long story." At Hadassah's look of alarm, she hastily said, "Her oldest daughter's been taken as a slave, temporarily. I'll explain once I get you some water.

"Girls, would you like to play in the courtyard? The donkey would be grateful for some hay. I haven't fed him yet."

When the girls disappeared and Hadassah settled on a stool, Jarah explained about Yael and the cost of the vineyard. "I don't know how they're going to come up with forty pieces of silver, Hadassah. They just get by. Naama was working on a rug, but she burnt her hands. She's finally starting to bend her fingers again. She's beside herself."

Hadassah's pleasure turned to distress. "It's our fault. Benjamin's the one who owes the debt."

"I didn't mean that at all!" Jarah exclaimed.

"Of course you didn't, but it's the truth all the same. And we don't have even half what Tobiah's demanding." She sighed and fell silent. "Wait! The Queen gave me a necklace a few moons before she died. If I can sell it, it would pay the debt."

"Who can afford royal jewelry in Jerusalem?"

"I don't know, but I'll take it to the street of the jewelers and find out," Hadassah promised.

"It would be better to let the men haggle over it."

"True. I'll talk to Benjamin tonight, but I hate to tell him. He's going to feel terrible about this whole mess."

"He deserves to know," Jarah said. "And it's not your responsibility to fix this. He's the one who chose to marry Judith." Noticing the troubled look on her friend's face and fearing she'd overstepped, Jarah changed the subject. "Tell me about Esther."

"I nursed her to a full recovery after the first illness. I massaged and exercised her right hand until she recovered its use, and then she practiced speaking until she could speak clearly again. We had a couple of good years, but when she fell down the tower steps, she failed quickly. She died five moons ago. I miss her."

"I'm sure you do. She was such a big part of your life that she'll always be with you," Jarah clasped her hand. "Your fine palace manners for example."

"I have to adjust to life outside the palace all over again. At least I fit in with Nehemiah."

"He worked in the palace?" Jarah asked.

"As one of the king's cupbearers. If he'd stayed, I think he would have become chief. The man who holds that position now is quite elderly and will need a successor soon. Of course, his appointment as Tirshatha is temporary, so who knows?" Hadassah surveyed the meal preparations. "How many are you cooking for?"

"Over a score of men and my own family."

"What can I do?"

"Praise Adonai! He sent you at the right moment. I didn't know how I was going to make enough, but here you are to help. I wanted to look for you this morning, but

120

there was all this work and the boys are taking turns sleeping. The men returned to the wall, so someone had to stay here.

"Let's prepare some leavened bread first." Jarah handed Hadassah a shallow, wooden bowl. "Have you heard anything reliable about when our enemy will attack?"

Hadassah's well-manicured hands fluttered nervously. "Nehemiah expects within the next three days. He has everyone whittling shafts for arrows because he says the archers will be our first defense. The men can whittle while they're waiting."

"I suspect Oren's working at a forge somewhere fashioning the tips. I wondered why he hadn't come back to get Jabin. Poor kid's exhausted, but I need to get him up soon."

"He won't be of any use if he's too tired. Maybe you should let him sleep as long as he can," Hadassah suggested.

"I'd like too, but Hoshea and Doran can't keep watch for as long as he can."

"The men will manage. Let your son get the rest he needs. He's a boy doing a man's job."

29

When Tobiah left Rabbah with the Arabians, the atmosphere in his home crackled like the air before a lightning storm. Abigail seemed ready to strike, and the servants and children avoided her.

Yael escaped to the marketplace to purchase produce for Cook. She slowed the gray nag to breathe in a whiff of freedom, but worry for David and the other Gibeonite laborers stalked her. She headed to Dael's shop.

Since Dael was showing a gray-haired matron his average stock, Yael sought comfort in her grandmother's fine rugs. She traced the wavy patterns in the wools and silks to find connections with both her em and softa.

Will I ever get to make a rug like this? Although her mother trained her to make and dye the threads, Yael had never knotted more than a few small pieces. Her hand dropped to her side when Dael approached.

"A bit of home?" he asked.

"Yes."

Dael dropped his voice. "My men made it to Jerusalem. There's a delay with the cargo, so I'm not expecting them back soon."

"You know Tobiah and Geshem started out yesterday. They're to meet the Samaritans tomorrow," Yael whispered.

"I knew they left. Our people will be ready for them," Dael answered.

"I hope so."

"The God of Israel does not slumber or sleep," Dael reminded her. He sighed. "I keep reciting the psalmist's words over and over to myself. My brother Benjamin's working on the wall too."

"I thought he lived in Susa."

"He used to, but he returned with the new governor. With the building skills he learned in Persepolis and Susa, he's invaluable to Nehemiah."

"I thought he worked the family vineyard," Yael said.

"He did. For several years. In Susa he started out working in the king's gardens, but there were lots of small building projects in the gardens. Then in Persepolis he worked on the gardens and the walls. As a youngster, he was always building."

Dael paused, looking into the distance, "Adonai gave him his heart's desire. I'm afraid I sent my brother down a painful detour by arranging his marriage into the vineyard owner's family."

"My em always said Adonai uses every experience of our lives. She's had a lot of bad experiences. King Xerxes executed her father before she was born. My dad dragged her away from civilization to the wilderness of Yehud."

"She's not fond of the vineyard?"

"She resented it at first, but I think it was growing on her. It's home now." Yael swallowed tears. "I don't know where they'll go if we lose it. Maybe Jerusalem. Mother can make rugs there. My abba and uncle will be disappointed, as will my brothers and sisters."

"And what of you?"

"I love setting new plants and seeing the vines send out shoots. I'd miss it, but I'll still settle in Gibeon with David, help his mother care for his invalid father. I'd see my family at Peshach if they move to Jerusalem."

A couple in fine linen robes entered, interrupting their conversation. "Go with God, Yael."

Yael remembered the lentils halfway back to Abigail's home. She returned to the market.

⌘⌘

Two days later a street urchin rattled the gate. "Go away," Yael shouted as she sat under the fig tree and kept all the children away from their cranky mother.

"I have an important message," the dirt-streaked boy insisted.

"From who?"

"The rug merchant."

Dael! Yael stood with the baby and crossed the courtyard to the iron gate.

"The soldiers are already returning. They've been sighted from the towers," the Syrian boy said.

The soldiers? "The Arabs?" Yael asked.

"Yes, and your master."

Yael didn't understand. It was too early for their return. They couldn't have reached Jerusalem and returned in such a short time.

The boy, who looked no older than Hymie, stuck a filthy hand through the gate.

"I'll get you something," Yael said, moving the baby farther out of his reach. She plucked a few ripe figs from the tree and dropped them into his hand. The child ran down the street.

124

Handing the baby to Noa, Yael hurried to find Abigail. She found her spinning goat hair into thread. "Dael sent another message. The men have been sighted from the towers. They're coming back."

Abigail abruptly stopped spinning. "There hasn't been time for them to attack Jerusalem and return. The city must be safe!" She buried her head in her hands and sobbed.

Yael tentatively approached and laid a hand on her mistress' back. Abigail wiped a hand on her robe and grasped Yael's. "They're saved!"

"But how?"

"I don't know. Maybe they found a fight on the way there, or Sanballat's men weren't ready. It doesn't matter," Abigail said.

"Tobiah will be in a foul mood."

Fear flickered over Abigail's face. "Probably. Run to let Cook know what's happening and help her prepare some of his favorite foods. I'll take the children to the neighbor's and leave one of the maids to watch them."

⌘⌘

When Tobiah whirled into the courtyard, his entourage had dwindled to a dozen men.

Abigail greeted him from the steps as the grooms rushed to deal with the mounts. Plastering a smile on her face, she said, "My husband, I'm glad you are safe. What news?"

"Those blasted Jews knew we were coming. Sanballat sent spies to find the lowest points of the wall. They found armed men lining the walls. Someone warned them. It was pointless to attack when they were on alert. You know

Jerusalem has the high ground. By the gods! Send me our best wine, Woman. I have guests."

30

I t's been a week, Oren. I don't know if the boys can work like this any longer," Jarah told her husband when he appeared to grab some hot bread and lentils for his dinner. "I don't know if you can either," she worried.

"I'll be back for a full night's sleep tonight," Oren said. "Nehemiah thinks the immediate danger is past. Sanballat's surprise attack was ruined, so the dogs slunk home. 'Course they'll try something else." He shoveled food into his mouth while standing at the hearth.

"Slow down. Sit down."

"Sorry," Oren said, sinking onto a stool. "It's been go, go, go as fast as I can, but you're right, I can slow down now. I have five others trained to make iron arrow tips, and the iron's almost gone, so there's not much use in hurrying."

"Can the boys all sleep at home tonight too?"

"I'm bringing Doran home. I'll see how the other two are. I think a lot of the men are going to collapse in whatever houses are available tonight. No one's been sleeping well at the wall. We'll still post a heavy watch and have a few men in reserve, but everyone's worn out."

"We need to get back to Gibeon in a week to harvest the grapes in Ariel's vineyard."

"I'll come with you unless there's more trouble here."

"Good. I was hoping you would."

"Some of the other men need to return for harvest too, so they can pay their creditors. Naama's family isn't the only one who owes money," Oren said, reaching for another piece of unleavened bread.

"I know. At least the others owe Jews and not a godless Ammonite."

"It doesn't seem to matter who's owed. A few other girls are serving their parents' creditors just like Yael."

"No! Why would Jews do that to each other?"

"Greed isn't limited to race, Jarah. It's embedded in the human heart."

"Ay. I suppose you're right, but I hate it."

"Our God does too."

⌘⌘

Jarah rejoiced when Oren brought the three boys back for dinner and a night's rest.

The next morning they gathered at the temple steps for a meeting called by the Tirshatha. Most men remained at the walls, but each group sent a few representatives.

"The immediate threat seems to be over, but we must remain vigilant," Nehemiah informed them. "From now on half the men should be armed and watching while the others work."

"This strategy is necessary, but will slow us down," Benjamin added. "I think we can close the breaches in our walls in two weeks. Nehemiah's household will work on the weak spots to the north and south since we're vulnerable there."

128

"Are there any issues I need to be aware of?" Nehemiah asked.

Oren stepped forward from the crowd. "Yes, Tirshatha. Several Gibeonite families, mine included, need to return for the grape harvest."

"We'll be sorry to see you go." Nehemiah turned to Jabin, Hoshea, and Doran. "You boys have been an immense help. Will you come back after harvest?"

"That's our plan," Oren answered. "And we don't have to leave until after the Sabbath."

"Good, I hope to see you before you leave. Anything else?"

"Yes. Tirshatha, some of the men are losing income in their trades because they've been building," Oren said. "Now there's the delay with the attack and half of us standing guard instead of building. They're worried they're going to be even farther behind on their payments."

"Payments?" Nehemiah asked.

"To creditors. Many didn't have coin for grain since the harvests haven't been plentiful, so to feed their families, they mortgaged their lands or houses. We also have taxes to pay, and sometimes a man has to borrow to pay what the king or governor says he owes," Oren explained.

Nehemiah looked thunderstruck. He cleared his throat. "I had no idea, but I'm going to investigate this matter. Assure the men I won't levy a governor's tax. Of course, we have to pay the royal tax.

"If anyone needs to attend to his own business, he should feel free to pursue his family's well-being. He can help on the wall as his business permits. All right, everyone, back to work."

31

Hadassah settled her head comfortably on her recumbent husband's chest, happy he was home for the night. "Matok, you heard Oren say many Jews owe creditors?"

"Yes, Nehemiah was unpleasantly surprised with that information." Benjamin ran his fingers through her thick, wavy hair, already losing the thread of the conversation. "I've missed you." His lips captured hers.

"I've missed you too," Hadassah said, surrendering to the pleasure of his hands on her body. She was almost asleep before she remembered her request.

"Benjamin," she whispered.

"Yes?"

"Tobiah's demanding payment for the vineyard."

"What?" Benjamin sat up. "Why's Tobiah involved? The land was Judith's dowry."

"He said he's working on her behalf."

Benjamin thought back to his encounter with Judith. "I doubt that. I told you about meeting her in the shop when I went to buy a gift for em. She's dripping with jewels. She doesn't care about her small dowry."

A taut silence pervaded their sleeping space until Benjamin continued. "The man's a liar. I'll talk to Ariel and try to sort this out."

"He's demanding fifty shekels. They were able to pay a few, but they still need forty to redeem Yael and hold onto the vineyard."

"He took their *daughter*?" Benjamin pictured his own sweet dark-haired girls.

"Many creditors are."

"Swine!"

"Benjamin!"

"Sorry. Now try to go to sleep. I'll take care of it." He curved his body protectively around Hadassah's and felt her relax, her breathing evening out. He wracked his brain for a way to contact Judith quickly, but harvest would be over in a few weeks. The swiftest courier couldn't reach Susa in the allotted time, never mind return. His mind spun until he drifted into an uneasy sleep during the third watch.

32

W e'll start harvesting tomorrow," Ariel told Naama as he accepted a cup of water.

"Will we have enough harvesters? Seems like half the village is in Jerusalem."

"It might take longer than usual, but we'll get it done." Ariel tweaked Ebin's nose. "You're going to help this year, aren't you, Son?"

"I wish Jarah's family were back. Those boys do a powerful lot of work," Raisa said wistfully.

"The Lord will provide," Ariel reminded his family.

Naama flexed her recovering fingers. *Sometimes He seems to move awfully slow.*

The next morning the family rose before dawn, ate some grain, and followed Ariel to the vineyard. Gili had already cut down half a row of grapes.

Naama and the children filled baskets with the bunches and carried them to the upper vat while the men used their knives to slice the grapes from the vines.

After a half dozen trips, Naama heard voices approaching on the path. She stood straight and kneaded sore back muscles, waiting to see who was coming. Menachem came into view with a child riding on his strong back. Tova held their middle son's hand, and thirteen-year-old Eliezer lugged a large pot of water.

"Shalom," the families greeted each other.

"Thank you for coming." Ariel clasped Menachem's shoulder.

"Oren's family will join us as soon as they've taken care of a few things. They returned at sundown yesterday," Menachem said.

"Praise Adonai!" Naama whispered.

"Some of Samuel's family will be out later today too," Menachem said.

Gili wiped sweat off his brow. "We have good neighbors."

"Let's get right to work," Ariel said. "When the sun gets high, we can rest and visit. Do you both have knives?"

Menachem and Eliezer brandished a pair of the iron utensils.

"Good, you take this row."

Naama wished she could talk to Tova as they worked, but they needed to oversee their children. Tova was gathering the grapes her men cut.

This was Eliezer's first year wielding a knife, and Tova kept stopping to watch him. She'd been hovering over him since he was a sickly baby. It was hard for her to let him become a man.

When Tova did gather grapes, she moved slowly. *Is something wrong?* She and her two sons weren't able to carry as quickly as Naama's children. Ebin was only picking up tiny bunches and popping an occasional juicy orb into his mouth. Naama couldn't blame him. She popped one into her own mouth and savored the juicy explosion.

133

When the families stopped for a water break, Naama asked, "How are you?"

Tova smiled. "Remember when we first met, at this vat?"

"We were both huge with our first pregnancies. I slipped stomping the grapes, and you helped me up," Naama said. "You were the only Gibeonite who treated me with any kindness after Ariel laid claim to his ancestor's vineyard."

"It's a good thing I did. You came to see me a few days later and realized I was in labor. You saved Eliezer's life when the midwife couldn't come."

Lost in memories of her earliest days in Gibeon, Naama almost missed the significance of their conversation. "Wait! You're pregnant?" she whispered.

"Yes. I'm a few months along."

"I hope you have a daughter this time."

"Me too. I see how close you are with your girls..." Tova faltered. "Have you heard any news of Yael?"

"David saw her less than a moon ago. She was in Jerusalem for a wedding. He said she looks well, but he wasn't able to talk with her much."

"That's something at least," Tova said sympathetically. "She'll be home soon, and you'll be having a wedding."

"Yes, you're right." Naama sighed as she returned to work.

We'll redeem Yael, but what about the vineyard? She calculated the produce from the first two rows with experienced eyes. A good harvest, but not exceptional, and her rug wasn't finished.

Ariel's words came back to her. "The Lord will provide." He had provided before, but this challenge was beyond any they'd ever faced.

134

Four screaming boys announced Jarah and Oren's arrival. Ariel immediately put them to work.

The three women kissed each other's cheeks.

"The boys have been perched on the walls of Jerusalem watching for the Samaritans and Arabs. They practically ran all the way back to Gibeon," Jarah said. "It's good to see them running and playing. And it's good to have Gedalya near again. Thank you for keeping him for us, Tova."

"He was no trouble, and I felt like I contributed to the effort on the wall. I'm relieved to have Menachem home," Tova answered.

"I'm glad to *be* home, and I wasn't gone nearly as long as the men. Naama, you'll never guess who I saw in Jerusalem."

"The Tirshatha?" Naama asked.

"Well, yes, but that's not who I meant. Hadassah's back!"

"No! She made that trip again?" Naama squealed.

"Yes, but she rode the whole way, and it took half the time. I met her two little girls. They're going to be beautiful, just like their mother.

"She wants you to send word to her at Nehemiah's the next time you're in Jerusalem. They're staying with him since Benjamin knows about wall construction. Even if they move to their own home, the Tirshatha's staff will know where to find them."

"The Feast of Tabernacles is coming up next month. I'll be able to see her," Naama said.

"The best news is she has a necklace Queen Esther gave her. She's trying to sell it, so she can give you the silver to redeem Yael and buy the vineyard."

"She's always been a true friend," Naama said, tears in her eyes. "Bless her!"

The women filled their baskets and filed up the path to the upper vat to deposit the grapes. "Is the threat of attack past?" Tova asked.

"It's hard to tell, but Nehemiah thinks so," Jarah answered. "Our enemies lost the element of surprise, so they didn't have enough men to attack the high ground of Jerusalem. Sanballat invited Nehemiah to a meeting shortly before we left. Nehemiah sent word he was busy."

"The nerve of those Samaritans!" Tova said.

Naama nervously eyed the wilderness to the northeast of the vineyard. "I'm glad there's some distance between us and Samaria."

33

nother messenger from Tobiah arrived at the east gate this afternoon," Shecaniah informed Nehemiah. "He left this papyrus for you."

Nehemiah sighed. "That's the third one in two weeks. I expect he's inviting me to a 'summit of the leaders of our area.' I wonder what location he suggests this time."

He took the scroll and skimmed it. "He suggests Hadid as a more convenient location. How many more polite ways can I say 'no'?"

"Maybe you should dispense with the courtesy," Benjamin suggested. "These men seem rather obtuse."

"You can write this one, Benjamin. Consult on the wording with your court-trained wife. I'm sure she can offer my excuses diplomatically, and I'll sign it tomorrow."

Nehemiah turned to Shecaniah, "Can you put the messenger up for the night and keep him from spying on us?"

"Some good wine should do the trick," Shecaniah said with a grin.

"Good thinking! Ask my cook for two jars. Thank you, Shecaniah."

Four days later, Shecaniah reappeared. "The messenger's back again, Tirshatha."

"Tell him I'm too busy for any meetings and send him back to his master. I'm not going to take the time to write to either Tobiah or Sanballat again," Nehemiah said, wiping sweat from his face.

"We've almost built up this area of the wall to the height of the piece Shallum and his daughters repaired. We're almost done, Shecaniah! And I'm not going to let those girls keep outbuilding me."

"Our enemies aren't going to give up."

"No, it doesn't seem they are, but this will give us a few more days to work. By the Feast of Tabernacles our city should be enclosed."

"I'll send the messenger on his way, my lord, but I'll delay him first to give you a bit more peace."

"Excellent idea!" Nehemiah tried to work faster, but he wasn't accustomed to back-breaking work. The heat of the day sapped his strength. He switched posts with one of the men standing guard and prayed they could finish before the Samaritans or Ammonites posed any serious threats.

He was watching from the wall two days later when a small cadre of mounted horsemen came into view. His gut told him they brought trouble.

He and Benjamin moved to the valley gate to meet them. A knot of men from Zanoah, repositioning rock nearby, gathered around him, spears and swords in hand.

A Samaritan courtier separated himself from the group and announced: "A letter from the great Sanballat, esteemed leader of Samaria, to the Tirshatha of Jerusalem.

"It's been reported, and confirmed by our friend Geshem, that you are rebuilding so you can rebel against his most magnificent King Artaxerxes and set yourself up as king. Prophets in Jerusalem are proclaiming you as king. It is our duty as loyal subjects to report these tidings to King Artaxerxes.

"Come meet with us." The courtier rolled up the scroll and looked at him expectantly.

Unsurprised by the political machinations of Samaria's governor, Nehemiah tried to gauge the Zanoahites' reaction. They tightened their grips on their weapons and looked at him expectantly.

"Nothing of the sort is going on here. You're making up tales. I'm too busy for this. Tell your master not to disturb me again," Nehemiah demanded.

"We've been here since the beginning of the work," the leader of the Zanoahites said, stepping forward. "I've heard none of this rubbish. Go back where you belong, and leave us in peace." His men rumbled their agreement, lifting their spears and swords.

"You're full of lies," one burly Jew shouted.

The riders whirled their mounts and cantered down the Jerusalem road. The Zanoahites returned to work.

"Do you think they'll send their misinformation to the king?" Benjamin asked.

"I don't know," Nehemiah answered.

"Do you think he'd believe them?"

"Perhaps. Kings keep a stranglehold on power, and they can't trust many people. Even the most loyal-seeming retainers betray their king when given the right motivation. I might have to return to assure him I'm working for his interests and not my own."

"Let's try to get this wall done first."

"Agreed," Nehemiah said, slapping Benjamin's back.

⌘⌘

Two days later, Samuel of Gibeon entered the valley gate and found Benjamin laboring with the men from Zanoah. "I'm glad I didn't have to search the city for you, Benjamin. Your mother has fallen and remains asleep. Your sister wants to know if you can come."

"Can you wait for me to inform Nehemiah so we can ride back together?"

"I'll check on the other men from Gibeon and see if there are any messages they want me to take back to their families. I'll return here and wait for you."

"Thank you, Samuel. I'll be as quick as I can."

Benjamin found Nehemiah inspecting the wall between the Horse Gate and East Gate. "My seventy-year-old em fell, and my sister's asking me to go to Gibeon. Samuel's waiting for me. I'll be back as soon as I can."

"Take all the time you need to be with your mother," Nehemiah responded. "You might not get this chance again. Almighty God brought you back to Yehud in time to offer her comfort." He beckoned two guards and instructed them to accompany Benjamin and Samuel.

If only I had time to organize a family visit... Em loved meeting her granddaughters and chatting with Hadassah, but she might not even recover consciousness. Benjamin winced. *I've just returned from Susa and would have been able to spend more time with her. And now this...*

Grateful for the king's mount, he trotted home, stuffed a robe and tunic into a bag, kissed Hadassah and the girls, and galloped away from Jerusalem with the other men.

140

34

When Gibeon's walls came into view, Yael nearly bounced off her horse in her excitement.

Johanan smiled at her. "Hold your horses, girl. We don't want you to get injured when you're this close to home."

Home! Was there ever such a lovely word? Yael grinned widely behind her veil but tried to curb her energy in order to heed Johanan's advice. If this fine Arabian caught her energy, they'd flash past the vineyard like the sirocco wind and she would be blown right off.

Had Tobiah sent word ahead? Probably not. He preferred the advantage of surprise. Her return would be a wonderful surprise...wouldn't it? Would there be enough coins to redeem her?

Their entourage swept up the harvested rows of her father's vineyard. When the dust settled, Yael could see her siblings huddled around her mother.

Sliding off her mount, she enclosed the group in a hug. When her siblings broke away, Yael caught sight of Naama's damaged hands. "Em, what happened?"

Her mother flexed her hands. "I touched a hot pot when the kitchen roof collapsed. They're healing, praise be Adonai." The light in her eyes died, and she looked away. "But I couldn't finish the rug. They were too stiff."

Panic filled Yael. The rug had been her one hope. If her em had finished it and been able to get a good price for it, then maybe there'd be enough shekels, but now...

Her eyes darted to her father and David who had appeared around the corner of the house. *Had her family gathered enough to redeem her?*

"Do you have my payment?" Tobiah demanded.

"We have twenty shekels. If you could give us one more year, we'll pay you the rest."

Yael sagged in relief against Raisa. *There was enough! But would her family go hungry until the next harvest?*

"The debt's been owed for nearly fourteen years. I'm calling it in," Tobiah answered. "You have until next week to vacate..."

Raisa gasped and clutched Ebin to her. Naama hid her face in her scarred hands.

Ariel inclined his head.

"Wait!" Yael trembled. "If I stayed with you, would that pay off the debt?" Beyond Tobiah, she saw a blotchy redness suffuse Johanan's face.

⌘⌘

"Come quickly," the guard summoned Benjamin from his mother's sickbed. "Tobiah and a dozen others just rode past town."

"What trouble is he trying to stir up out here?" the other grumbled.

Benjamin thought for only a moment. "I know exactly where he's headed. Follow me!" He could imagine his men's confusion as they mounted, exited a hidden gate at the back of town and headed past several vineyards. He didn't have time to explain about the land he'd formerly owned as part of his wife's dowry.

They burst into the packed dirt area surrounding his erstwhile home, startling the tense-looking occupants and a gloating Tobiah. "I believe your business is with me," Benjamin boomed.

"Ahh, the dog who divorced my sister," Tobiah sneered.

Yael recognized Benjamin from her girlhood. Yet he was different. His features were no longer etched with despair, but determination.

"Judith and I have settled our differences. Why are you here?" Benjamin asked.

"Of course you'd say that. How could you possibly have communicated with my sister about her dowry?"

"I lived in Susa. She's a rich merchant's wife. I'm sure she's not interested in a paltry forty coins."

"You have a document showing proof of payment?" Tobiah asked.

"No."

Tobiah drew a tablet from his bag. "Until I see proof nullifying this dowry agreement, this is still in effect." He gestured toward Ariel's family. "In the meantime, they can stay. I'll take the girl as collateral."

"It could take half a year to send and receive a message," Benjamin protested.

"When you hear from my sister, you know where to find me." Tobiah wheeled his horse.

Johanan pointed to the desolate hills beyond the vineyard. "We'll prepare a meal and rest for an hour. Yael can eat with her family."

Tobiah glowered but disappeared over a rise, followed by his son and servants.

Touched by Johanan's boldness in standing up to his father to extend her a kindness, Yael remained rooted to the plot causing her family's distress. When Naama started to sob, she wrapped her arms around her em, shocked to feel bones rather than her mother's soft curves.

"You should be marrying after the harvest. That wicked, wicked man!" Naama balled her fists and rocked back and forth.

"Everything will work out. Our God sees, and He will answer our cries." Yael tried to speak with more confidence than she felt.

Naama pressed a trembling hand to her mouth and breathed deeply until she quieted. "Go, you should be with your betrothed. I'll be all right." With a shuddering breath, she gave Yael a gentle push toward David.

He caught her small hands in his big, work-roughened ones. "I'm waiting for you, as long as it takes. Our vines are thriving. They're our future."

"Thank you," Yael whispered, eyes downcast.

David tensed. "Has that man touched you?"

"No, no. I'm careful, very careful."

"But they didn't bring another woman while you're traveling. That's not good."

"I'm only a servant. He's not treating me like kin. Abigail and Johanan are good to me, kind and considerate. Johanan watches out for me."

"We all miss you and your sunny ways. It's been somber around here. And with the threat to Jerusalem..."

Yael looked up. "Abigail and I heard their plans. We sent word by way of Benjamin's brother's caravan."

"You were part of that?" David's deep brown eyes warmed with approval.

144

"A small part. There are other Jews in Rabbah," Yael looked around the vineyard. "Rabbah's not home, but it's not such a bad place. It doesn't get as hot."

"Don't get too used to it."

"No, I..." Yael was interrupted by her sister bringing a basket of flat bread. "Let's eat with my family. I don't have much time."

"Of course," David agreed. "But I hardly have an appetite. I just want to sit and look at you."

Yael blushed. "If you don't eat now, your stomach will be rumbling later."

"For heaven's sake, you can nibble *and* look," Raisa blurted. "Both of you come into the shade with the rest of us."

Even with everyone chattering non-stop, Yael couldn't catch up on all the family and village news before Johanan appeared around the corner of the house, "It's time, Yael."

Yael quickly embraced her family. Ariel held the horse while David helped her mount. "I'll be home soon," she said, pushing the words past the lump in her throat.

"We pray for God's blessing on you every day, Yael. Go with God," Ariel answered.

⌘⌘

"I'm sorry, my friends," Benjamin said as Naama dejectedly watched her daughter disappear.

"This vineyard's been nothin' but trouble," Naama muttered as she disappeared into the house.

Ariel looked apologetically at Benjamin. "We still have a home. If you hadn't arrived when you did..." He gestured toward his youngsters. "We'd be homeless, or Yael would be lost to us forever. Adonai brought you, not a moment too late."

David asked, "How long will it take to get proof in writing that the debt's been paid?"

"Four months at best, if I catch couriers at the right times."

"What a bull-headed thug! What right does he have to collect on behalf of his sister?" David raged.

"Since Judith and I settled the matter, none. However, meddling in others' business is Tobiah's strong suit," Benjamin said.

Ariel offered both men cups of wine. "Benjamin, we never paid you for your portion of the vineyard."

Benjamin swirled and sniffed the liquid. "This has a sweet aroma. Thank you for the sample."

He sipped with pleasure. "Although I enjoy the finished product, I agree with Naama about the vineyard. It's caused me untold heartache. If you want to take on this troublesome piece of dirt, it's yours."

"That's too generous. We can at least bring you wine after every harvest."

Benjamin nodded as he returned the cup. "Hadassah and I would appreciate the new wine. I'll agree to two jugs."

He swung up on his fine Arabian. "If this horse didn't belong to King Artaxerxes, I would have offered him to Tobiah. As soon as I return to Jerusalem, I'll try to arrange for a messenger. Hanani is due to arrive soon. He would be a reliable man for this job." He rode off, trailed by the guards.

After their visitors disappeared on their respective roads, David gazed in the direction Yael had ridden. "That Tobiah seems to have a powerful liking for my Yael."

Yael gave her mare its head as she twisted to look back at the only home she'd ever known. The vines she and David had planted two years ago had doubled in thickness. The new vines transplanted by Raisa and David were spindly and fragile, but the leaves appeared healthy.

Adonai, I beg you—bring me home before they bud, and let me wed before the next harvest. After being freed from Tobiah, she would never leave Yehud again.

The days riding to Rabbah wore Yael down. She had known she might not be redeemed, but...she had hoped. How much longer would she be forced to live away from her family? She developed a cough and weakened so she could barely stay on her mount.

Just like her initial arrival, her legs wouldn't support her after she dismounted in Tobiah's courtyard. Johanan and a groom carried her to a pallet, and Abigail brought her water and tried to make her comfortable. Despair receded as blessed sleep claimed her.

She faded in and out of fevered dreams. Sometimes voices whispered outside her door. "She's always been a healthy young woman. Why does she have a fever?" a male asked.

"Her hopes were crushed. Her spirit's wounded," a motherly voice responded.

"Would taking her out of the city to the goatherd's camp help?"

"Maybe when she's stronger, but it's going to be cold soon. We'll be able to keep her warm here in the house. Your wife would also do better in the city for the winter."

"Eden...yes, of course you're right. I'll go get her and bring her back, as soon as I know Yael's out of danger."

Water dripped into Yael's parched mouth, and gentle hands sponged her with cool cloths. She wanted to open her eyes, see who the speakers were. Their names hovered just out of reach of her memory. She returned to fevered dreams.

Three days later she woke with the sun on her face and recognized Abigail smiling down at her as she dribbled broth into Yael's mouth. "Don't try to talk just yet," she soothed. "You'll end up coughing. We need to get as much broth into you as possible. Cook will be glad to see an empty bowl."

Strength began to flow through Yael's body as she slowly swallowed the soup. Each mouthful became easier as the moisture revitalized the dry muscles. Abigail left to replenish the bowl, but Yael's eyelids drooped and closed against her will.

⌘⌘

"She's better now?" Johanan asked his mother as he searched Yael's sleeping face for any tinge of health or color. "She doesn't look any better."

"She ate an entire bowl of broth. I believe she's going to recover."

"I'll go find the herds tomorrow."

"You still have time today."

"I know, but it's not getting cold yet, so I can wait another day...just to make sure."

Abigail laid a gentle hand on her son's arm. "She's come to mean much to both of us, but it's just for a short time. By next harvest..."

Johanan sighed. "I could have let her go this last time, but I'm not sure I can now. Seeing her so sick..."

148

He swallowed hard and continued. "She never complains about being forced away from everything she knows and loves."

Johanan ran his hands through his thick black hair. "Her family's vineyard is a sorry patch of dust, and it's supporting more and more people. If she returns, she's destined to a life of poverty. Her mother looks older than you, but I know she's ten years younger. I don't want that to happen to Yael."

"So you'd force her to remain?"

"No! I'm not my father, but...I could give her a choice."

"You haven't given Eden enough time, Johanan."

"Eden is a spoiled, yammering child."

"She'll mature."

"Maybe. Until then I'd like to stay away."

"Bring Eden here for the winter. Spend as much time as you can out with the herds."

Johanan's shoulders sagged. "But Yael..."

"I'll watch out for Yael. She's a hard worker, but I won't give her too much to do before she's fully recovered." Abigail dipped a cloth in water and wiped Yael's face.

"Try to convince your father to go with you. He's been asking why I'm nursing her back to health. He won't want her to 'lie around and do nothing' while I pick up extra work."

"What did you tell him?"

"A dead servant isn't of any use. She's diligent and trustworthy, and I want her to be able to help with the children again." Abigail paused. "But of course it's more. I suppose I love her for the same reasons you do."

"Is it that obvious?"

"Only to a mother's eyes, though if you're not careful your wife *will* notice. She could make life miserable for Yael."

"I'll stay away from Yael then."

"Spend a few weeks with your wife in the fields before you bring her here for the winter. If you can get her with child, the pregnancy will take most of her attention. It will be easier for everyone."

35

Judith scowled as she stared in disbelief at the heavy cedar gates. The city she had last seen as a pile of rubble had metal-bound gates set in stout stone walls. And they were closed!

Ctesias was charging around like an angry bull, dispatching servants to other gates. "Bribe our way in if you have to." He galloped off, cursing, to search for a way into Jerusalem.

The caravan master Basim approached Judith apologetically. "There weren't any walls or gates the last time we were here. Would you like to dismount while we wait?" He assisted her down from her white mare.

"They have to let us merchants in eventually. Let me find you a rug so you can rest in the shade." He hurried away, calling for the caravan boys to locate rugs for their mistress.

Rumors abounded at the caravansaries about the Jews rebuilding their walls. It was considered a marvel. Their god hadn't forgotten them after all.

Everyone also spoke reverently of the new Tirshatha, Nehemiah. He came from obscurity as the king's cupbearer to the governorship of Yehud and was outwitting the scoundrels Sanballat and Tobiah.

Laughter and derision for the two leaders followed those comments, except in Samaria and Ammon. Inside their respective countries, lengthy excuses were concocted for Sanballat and Tobiah's failures.

The comments about Tobiah stung, but Judith amused herself by baiting the Samaritan women to see what outlandish tales they invented to exonerate Sanballat.

Judith was not amused now. Sasha arranged a small, crimson rug in the shade of a fig tree, and Judith reclined, attempting to keep her robe out of the dust. When her legs prickled from their unnatural position, she gave up on cleanliness and found a more comfortable position.

At the sixth hour, a slave brought cool water and grapes. "Has anyone discovered why the gates are still closed?" Judith asked him.

"No, mistress, but there are many watchmen on the walls, which is odd since we saw no signs of trouble."

Judith's lip curled in derision. "We didn't hear of any threats, even in Rabbah or Samaria. These Jews are scared of their own shadows."

"I'll let you hear as soon as we learn anything, mistress."

"Thank you." Judith ate in a leisurely manner and stretched out for a rest. When she woke, the sun was sinking, and a servant crouched nearby.

"It's their holy day," he informed her. "Their Tirshatha has commanded they keep the gates closed and refrain from trade. We'll be able to enter and find shelter after sunset."

"Good. I don't want to be sleeping out here tonight. Has your master returned?"

"Ctesias is at the front of the caravan with Basim." Since the servant looked a bit scared, Judith decided Ctesias' foul mood had not improved and stayed where she was.

The heavy gates creaked open at sunset, and Ctesias' caravan jostled their way into the city with others delayed by the Jewish Sabbath. Basim guided them to the closest lodgings, a decrepit stone inn.

Judith wearily sank onto a plush rug brought from the caravan. "Will that be all, mistress?" one of the servants asked.

"Make sure Sasha brings up a pitcher of water."

After the servants left, Judith took in her dismal, cramped room. Ctesias was downstairs drinking with a few of the businessmen he'd been able to get hold of at the late hour. He had assured her they would find better quarters tomorrow, but she told him the lodgings weren't important if their business could be conducted quickly. Now she doubted her decision.

As long as there aren't any rodents, I can put up with this for a night or two. We can stop over in a more civilized place on the way home, visit family in Rabbah, shop in Damascus. Yes, that's perfect. As soon as I take care of my offering at the temple.

36

Judith rose early so she could attend the morning sacrifice. Two guards escorted her to the temple mount. One waited at the gate to the court of the Gentiles while the other went in search of a perfect ram from the animal sellers.

Judith positioned herself in the court of the Gentiles so she could see the bronze altar, which sat on a raised platform. A priest in bright blue robes expertly sacrificed a bleating lamb. She recoiled at the memory of the metal blade in her hand cutting off the life of her baby daughter.

Please accept my sacrifice and remove these images from my mind, God of Israel.

Dressed as an Israeli matron, Judith knew she could pass the woven stick wall dividing the Gentile's court from the Jewish women's, but it didn't seem right when she was asking for forgiveness. She stayed in the outer court.

The guard returned with a ram. Judith nodded in approval and set her hand on the animal's head. The guard led it to a Levite and pointed back to Judith.

The Levite headed out of sight but reappeared near the altar. He handed the rope to the priest and they spoke briefly. Then the Levite positioned the ram on the bronze grate and the priest slaughtered Judith's offering.

Judith released a repressed breath and bowed her head, searching for peace. She remained in this humble posture, waiting for....absolution? A sign of some sort?

"Shalom," a kindly voice intoned.

Looking up, Judith saw the blue-robed priest standing in front of her. His face bore the lines of middle age. His brown eyes were probing but serene. "My name is Ezra. It was a fine sacrifice, daughter. I have a message for you."

Hope flooded Judith.

"Go and do works worthy of repentance."

Of course, the key to being free of her past was...living a different life in the future. But how does this man know me? I don't remember him from when I worshipped with Benjamin. Wait! Ezra? This man mandated the divorces that ripped apart my family.

"I don't know you or the sin you've come to be forgiven of, but forgiveness requires repentance on your part. Then the Almighty does His part and covers your wrongdoing."

Stunned, Judith mumbled, "I will. Thank you." She turned to go.

"May the God of peace shine on you, on your coming and going," the priest blessed.

37

In a quiet courtyard of the inn, usually reserved for the innkeeper's family, Judith was turning the priest's words over in her mind when Sasha interrupted, "You have a visitor, mistress."

Who could be visiting me here?

"Show him, or her, in."

"Your caller is a Jewish matron, but she didn't leave her name."

A woman? Maybe Tova, but it's not a festival, so I don't know why she'd be in Jerusalem.

As soon as the woman made a graceful entrance, Judith knew her identity though they'd never met.

"Shalom, Judith, wife of Ctesias," the beauty began in a gentle tone.

"Shalom, Hadassah, wife of Benjamin," Judith answered. She had always considered her own voice mellifluous, but it seemed strident by comparison.

Covering her discomfort, she gestured to a stool, "Please, sit." Judith perched warily on a bench, mind racing.

Hadassah cleared her throat. "How was your journey?"

"Slow but prosperous, thank you."

A long silence stretched as Hadassah waited for more details. When Judith remained reticent, Hadassah said, "I'll come right to the point. I understand my husband owes you a debt for your vineyard dowry.

"We don't have coin, but would you accept this in payment?" Hadassah drew a soft pouch from her robes and removed an exquisite necklace.

Judith gasped as she took the gold and emerald piece and fingered the gems. "I've never seen such fine work."

"It belonged to Queen Esther. She gave it to me for my service."

Judith closed her eyes. *A queen's jewels! I could be the envy of all my friends. This would even impress Ctesias.* But the priest's words rang in her ears, "Go and do works worthy of repentance."

"I can't accept," she said, a bit curtly, handing the jewelry back.

Hadassah looked distressed. "Please, your brother Tobiah is demanding payment for the vineyard in your name. He's taken Naama's oldest child as a slave and is threatening to take their livelihood. There's no way they can pay."

Prickles of hate heated Judith's neck at the mention of the family who had claimed her vineyard as their ancestral inheritance, but then memories sluiced over her like icy water. Naama, wailing in the vineyard for her dead firstborn son, while Judith clutched healthy, beautiful Hen. Naama, bent over Tova, delivering Eliezer and rubbing life into his tiny blue body.

Why is Tobiah collecting my dowry? I've never been interested in payment.

"How much is he demanding?" Judith asked.

"Fifty shekels."

I took so much more from Benjamin than silver.

"Harvest was fair this year, nothing special," Hadassah continued. "There are seven of them, and now they have nowhere to go. Yael, the one Tobiah enslaved, is betrothed."

Judith had to admit Naama was a good woman. *"Works worthy of repentance"* whispered through her mind.

"The debt is paid," Judith said slowly, deliberately. "I'll call a scribe to record its cancellation." She ignored Hadassah's effusive thanks, rising from the bench and pacing past a couple of potted fruit trees. "I think I'd like to see the vineyard one more time, but the villagers wouldn't be happy to see me. Last I knew they wanted to stone me."

"Do you think it's wise to go back?"

"No one would call me wise," Judith said wryly, "but in order to be free, sometimes you have to revisit the scene of your deepest regrets. I'll never have this chance again. Trekking here from Susa isn't something I want to do again."

"I've made the trip three times, and I don't want to travel it again either," Hadassah agreed.

"Benjamin and I have horses the king lent us. He's already in Gibeon visiting his mother. Would you like me to go with you, Judith? We could leave later this morning and be there before nightfall."

"Yes, that should work. My servants will pack a tent and supplies. We'll take a couple of the caravan's guards while my husband finishes his business here in the city."

158

"Can you meet me at the Mishneh Gate when the sun is at its height?" Hadassah asked.

"I'll be there as soon as I make all the arrangements. It shouldn't take me long."

"I need to take my daughters to my sister."

Judith tamped down a flicker of irritation. "I'll wait."

38

The sun skimmed the horizon as the silent travelers entered the gates of Gibeon. Hadassah headed to Benjamin's family home so he could accompany them to the vineyard.

While the guards dismounted to stretch their legs, Judith descended the spiraling stairs with Sasha to fill their goatskins with sweet spring water. She'd always been intrigued with Gibeon's water source though she never liked the steep, spiral descent.

Hadassah and Benjamin were waiting when the women reemerged from the well.

"We meet again," Benjamin said to Judith. "I'm glad you're here to put an end to the threat against Ariel and Gili's livelihood. Under our law, I do owe you payment. Could I...?"

"Since we met at my shop, I've believed our debts to each other were canceled," Judith interrupted.

Benjamin inclined his head, "Thank you, Judith."

They remounted and exited the city through a narrow gate. A goat barreled toward them with two small boys in hot pursuit. Judith's horse sidestepped and she struck her shoulder hard against the stone. Pain stole her breath, but she kept her seat.

"Judith, are you all right?" Hadassah asked as Benjamin yelled after the boys to be more careful.

"I...I think so. There's no blood," she said as Sasha tried to assess the damage through several layers of clothing. Pouring cold spring water on a loose piece of fabric eased Judith's discomfort, but the rag was difficult to hold in place while riding. "Let's continue on foot, so I can hold this in place. It's not much farther."

Looking somber, Benjamin rode ahead to inform Ariel's family of their imminent arrival. The three women walked, flanked by Judith's mounted guards leading the other horses.

As the grape vines came into view, memories pressed down on Judith. *What is Benjamin remembering? This place became full of pain for both of us.*

But it all happened more than ten years ago. I'm here to put it all to rest.

Benjamin returned on foot to lead the entourage along the packed dirt path. The fall rains would turn it into mud soon. The women would be fighting to keep their floors clean. How thankful Judith was to be done with the mud, both in Rabbah and Gibeon. The slaves cleaned it off the floors in her Susa home.

Shoulder aching, she longed for home--a good bath, clean bed, silk robes. But tonight would be spent in primitive surroundings.

Ahead, she saw Ariel, Gili, a young man, and Naama, flanked by a skinny girl and several smaller boys.

"Shalom," Ariel greeted them.

"Raisa, fetch our guests some water," Naama said. Her hospitality seemed strained.

She's remembering how I fought them for the vineyard, and what I did to Hen.

"We're surprised to see you in Yehud, Judith," Ariel began. "Don't you live in Susa?"

"Yes, but I made the journey with one of my husband's merchant caravans. Hadassah found me today and told me my brother's demanding payment for my dowry."

"You weren't aware?"

"No, I'm as surprised as you were. I haven't heard from Tobiah for two years or more. I spoke with Benjamin earlier this year before he left Susa. Our debts are settled. Nothing is owed me for this vineyard."

"So Yael was taken for nothing?" the young man bristled.

"This is David, Yael's betrothed," Ariel said.

"I'm sorry for the pain this has caused you. There was no reason for Tobiah to take your intended bride."

I hope his intended bride still has her virtue intact.

"I'm sure it's been a long day. Why don't you women go inside?" Ariel suggested.

The newcomers followed Naama and her children into a small kitchen. "You've made many improvements to your home," Judith said.

"Well, yes, this is the most recent. Our kitchen was rebuilt this year." Naama gestured to some stools and flexed her fingers.

Hadassah and Judith sat while Sasha stood behind her mistress. Naama and Raisa positioned a bench and settled on it.

Uncertain how to fill the silence, Judith rubbed her sore shoulder.

Sasha asked, "Could I have a dipperful of water?"

162

"Certainly," Naama said. The water pitcher is in the corner. Help yourself to as much as you'd like."

As the other women watched, Sasha took a small drink and then dampened the compress and handed it to Judith.

"Are you hurt?" Naama asked. "Maybe I have something to help. Is it a burn, bump, or bruise?"

"I'm not sure. It happened on our way out of Gibeon, and we couldn't get a good look."

Naama shooed her boys out, and Sasha gently peeled back the linen robe.

"A bit of a scrape that will turn into a bruise," Naama declared. "Not a lot we can do, but let's try some ointment. May I press on it, make sure it's not dislocated?"

Judith nodded and explained her mishap.

Naama probed lightly, then washed it with tepid water, patted it dry, and applied fragrant salve. "Rest now. You may not want to ride tomorrow."

"What did you say?"

"Riding might aggravate it, but you can stay a day or two," Naama assured her.

"No, before that?"

Naama looked confused.

Hadassah intervened. "Naama said 'Rest now.' Do you want to lie down, Judith?"

"Yes, that's what she said, and I've heard it said just that way."

Naama and Hadassah stared at her as if she'd taken leave of her senses.

"Recently. Not when I lived here." Judith closed her eyes to think.

"Mistress, she sounds like the Persian midwife who attended you earlier this year," Sasha offered.

"Of course! Artystone," Judith remembered.

"My em? You've seen my em? I haven't heard from her for so long!" Naama said. "How is she? How did she look?"

"She's well. Your voices are alike, Naama. You have the same soothing way of speaking. It came back to me when you said 'Rest now.'"

The light drained from Naama's face. "Your babe?"

"Born too early to survive. I fell down some steps..."

"Everyone knows that bad boy *knocked* you down the steps, Mistress," Sasha said heatedly.

"We're sorry, Judith," Hadassah said.

"Thank you." Judith swallowed hard. "I figure I deserve it, after what I did to Hen."

She looked down, wringing the rag. "That's really why I came to Jerusalem—to make amends. I'm sure I angered Adonai when I...did what I did. I came to offer Him a sacrifice, and then Hadassah found me and told me what was going on with Tobiah.

"The priest told me to 'do works worthy of repentance.' I *can* make things right with your vineyard, so I will."

"I don't think Adonai punishes us like that," Hadassah said quietly. "But He's always pleased with repentance."

"Bad things happen, whether you do what's right or not," Naama added. "I suppose Adonai uses bad things to get our attention. I'm so glad you were listening, Judith. Now we can bring Yael home."

39

Yael soaked up the sunshine as she sat on a limestone bench in Tobiah's courtyard. Her cough had subsided after a week, but her strength hadn't returned. Occasionally she watched the children, but mostly she rested and ate the nourishing soups Cook prepared for her.

Birdsong and the humming of insects filled the courtyard with peace. The younger children and Abigail were napping, and the older ones were working with Cook. A groom brushed the horses.

Johanan, Eden, and Tobiah would return to the main house to winter. There wouldn't be many more days like this. Yael closed her eyes.

Her nap ended with a vicious tug yanking her to her feet. "You lazy good-for-nothin'," Tobiah yelled in her face.

Tears pricked Yael's eyes at the pain in her arm. She started to cough in his face. Tobiah released her abruptly, and Yael tumbled onto the rough pavers and scrambled backwards, scraping her hands.

"Father, she's been sick," Johanan sprang between Yael and her attacker.

"That was weeks ago! Get out of my way, boy!"

"No! You won't beat her."

Tobiah laughed. "She's my servant. I'll do what I want."

Abigail appeared at the back door. "You're home!" she tried to infuse a welcome into her voice. "Come have some cold water and fruit while Cook prepares a meal."

"I'm busy, woman," Tobiah growled.

Without taking his eyes off his father, Johanan said, "And here I thought you acquired her to serve mother. Are you dissatisfied with Yael's work, Mother?"

"No, but she's just becoming useful again. She was at death's door, Tobiah. I beg you not to put her out of work for any longer." Abigail edged down the steps toward her husband.

"She's useless! I'll put her out of her misery and go back for one of her sisters."

Panic flooded Yael. Tobiah had backed her up against the wall of the stable. The madman meant to kill her and enslave her sister!

She coughed until she choked, tears streaming down her face. *Adonai Elohim, save me.*

"I claim her as my concubine. Her bride price can be her family's vineyard," Johanan yelled.

Yael almost stopped breathing. She gasped for breath and shook her head to clear her ears. *What?? Surely she didn't hear correctly.*

Tobiah glared at her. Abigail sidled up to him and gently placed a hand on his arm. He shook it off.

"Fine. If you want the sickly little wench, take her. Just get her out of my sight. I don't want her infecting the rest of the family." He stalked into the house, Abigail trailing behind.

Johanan watched him warily, and then breathed in relief, until his eyes met his wife's. Eden was still sitting on her horse. Her eyes were wide with reproach.

She guided the horse to him, and he caught the harness. "How dare you! You've not fulfilled your year with me," she hissed. "And for what? A peasant who's on the verge of death?"

Wearily, Johanan shook his head. "We'll discuss this later, Eden. Right now I need to get Yael to safety. I'll take her back out to the goat camp.

"Don't unpack my tent," he instructed the groom. "Get me a fresh mount."

While the groom complied, Johanan knelt before Yael, who could only look at him in shock. He gently wiped her face and called for some water. After she sipped it, she stopped coughing but breathed shallowly, watching him with huge eyes.

"Noa, go pack Yael's bag for her," Johanan told his younger sister.

"She's not a servant," Eden said contemptuously.

"No but she's a good girl." Johanan smiled at Noa. "And unless someone packs Yael's things, I'll have to take your packed bags back with me."

Noa scampered off, while Johanan helped Yael back to the bench. He poured water over her bloody hands and tenderly dried them while his wife stared. "Go in the house, Eden. I'll be back in a few days."

Johanan swung up on a large bay and walked her over to Yael, motioning for Yael to step up on the rock to mount in front of him.

Yael shrank back. "Please, I can ride by myself, if it's not too far."

167

"You don't look very strong, Yael, but I guess it would be better to ride separately." Johanan refilled waterskins while the groom brought Yael a small black mare.

Neither of them spoke as they headed to the marketplace for vegetables and grain. Johanan led two donkeys loaded with the tent and other supplies.

While Johanan shopped, Yael's thoughts swirled like the Jordan in flood. *Johanan knows I'm betrothed, but he claimed me as his concubine. He wants the vineyard to belong to my family as his gift, but Benjamin said we already own it. Judith just needs to send written proof.*

And I belong to David. Will Johanan take me anyway? He doesn't seem like that kind of man.

They didn't travel far outside Rabbah before weariness and an aching head left her doubled over and clinging to her mare's neck. Johanan rode beside her.

After a *parasang* he said, "You're going to fall, Yael. I'd stop and camp here but it wouldn't be safe. We could try to hide in an outcrop but we couldn't have a fire, and you need to be kept warm. Stop being stubborn and come ride with me."

Tears slipped down Yael's face.

"I'm not going to force you. I wanted to protect you. I've seen my father beat slaves to death. I couldn't let him hurt you."

Yael nodded dumbly and guided her horse close to Johanan. She slid her leg over her mount and he plucked her off as if she were a sack of grain and settled her in front of him. Exhausted, she relaxed into his chest and was lulled to sleep.

The air had cooled and stars appeared when she woke to Johanan hailing the goatherds. A skinny male of her age ran to take the donkeys. She slid off the bay, and Johanan wearily dismounted and nudged her toward the fire.

168

Removing his horse's bridle, he called to the cook. "I'm sorry for the late notice, but can you stretch a meal for two more? You'll find bread and fruit in the large sack on the dark gray donkey."

The white-haired man stirring the stew nodded and rummaged through the pack Skinny dropped in front of him. Two younger goatherds unloaded the beasts and started pitching Johanan's tent.

Yael sank down on the non-smoky side of the fire, sniffing appreciatively. When her stomach growled loudly, Johanan disappeared into one of the tents. He quickly reappeared with a wooden bowl, scooped broth into it, and handed it to her.

Yael tipped it to her mouth and regained some life as the warmth soothed her throat and satisfied her hunger pangs.

After the men had eaten, the goatherds slunk into the darkness to their tasks or beds.

Johanan crouched, studying her face in the flickering firelight. "I love you, Yael," he said, brushing the back of his hand against the smoothness of her cheek. "I didn't realize how much until you were sick. We almost lost you."

"But I'm committed to David. We grew up together."

Johanan took her hand and rubbed his thumb over her fingers. "Sometimes couples break off a betrothal. There would be no shame for either of you, given the circumstances.

"David would have done anything to protect you if he were here today, but he wasn't. My father wouldn't have listened to him anyway. He probably would have killed both of you. David would want you to live, Yael, not be slaughtered."

"But I'm so close to going home. Benjamin said the vineyard's paid for. All we need is written proof."

169

"It could take six moons for the proof to arrive. And something could happen in the meantime. If Judith succumbs to an illness or changes her mind and the transaction wasn't recorded..."

Yael looked at him in horror. "I never considered any of that," she whispered, looking down at their linked hands.

"Do you think you could come to love me? I know you're a loyal soul, but we could have a long life together," Johanan pleaded.

"Your father wanted to kill me. I'm not looking at a long life if I stay here. And you're right—I am loyal, to my home and my family as well as the man I've loved for years."

"You have time to think about it. We can hide here, though we'll have to return to Rabbah before it gets too cold. I don't want you to get sick again."

Yael tried to pull her thoughts together. "You honor me with your offer, Johanan. Thank you for protecting me from your father today."

"I'll sleep in another tent tonight. You take my tent. There's a thick rug and plenty of blankets. Keep yourself warm."

So you don't have to. A concubine wasn't honored with a marriage ceremony. She simply began sharing her husband's bed. Heat flooded Yael. "I'll be fine," she croaked.

"Let me know if you need anything. I will take care of you, Yael." The passion in Johanan's eyes added threat to his promise.

Rising on shaky limbs, Yael stood with as much dignity as possible and retired before Johanan's passion overruled his good sense.

170

Once in the tent, she laid out the rug and piled every blanket she could find to form a bed. She took her extra cloak from her bag and pulled it around her body. It *was* cool away from the fire. Tomorrow there would be ice crystallized on the dead grass.

Why does this man desire me? He has Eden, who's far prettier. Not much fun to be around though, with all her whining. Em always said not to speak with words that become a constant drip. Yael's thoughts became hazy as her bed warmed and sleep claimed her.

40

S end word to all the men to meet in front of the Water Gate," Nehemiah instructed his servants. "Our work is done. It's time for them to go home."

Within an hour, most of the citizens of Jerusalem and the other Israelites who came to build stood in the large courtyard inside the Water Gate.

Nehemiah stepped forward, and the crowd quieted. "In spite of the opposition of our enemies, the Almighty God has looked on us with favor and we've accomplished what we set out to do, in just fifty-two days. The wall around our city is complete."

The Israelites roared their approval.

Nehemiah continued, "I know you're tired. You've put more effort into this wall than I ever thought possible. And our enemies—they said it couldn't be done. When they hear of our feat, they *will* know there is a God in Israel.

"Now go to your homes, set things in order, and then bring your families back on the first of Tishri to see what God has raised up through you.

"If you leave through this gate, my servants have figs to give you for your journey home. Stay in groups and travel safely. Shalom."

Most of the departing Jews had brought their few belongings and immediately thronged out the gate, taking handfuls of fruit from huge baskets.

⌘⌘

A score of men from Gibeon arrived in the city to shouts of welcome from their women and children. Jarah sent Jabin to Ariel's vineyard with news of the assembly.

"It's done," Jabin panted as he ran up to Ariel, Gili, and David. "The wall...it's complete. Everyone is invited to Jerusalem for the first of Tishri."

"Great news. Let's go tell the women," Ariel responded. "Come have a drink, Jabin, and tell us all again."

After Jabin recounted the news for Naama and Judith, Raisa danced Ebin around in a circle. The other little boys joined in.

"We'll leave in two days," Ariel announced. "Everyone can go see the wall. Will you be well enough to travel, Judith?"

"Yes, but if I feel well enough, I'll return tomorrow. Ctesias will wonder about my delay. Thank you for your hospitality while my shoulder healed."

"Having you here has been a blessing," Ariel assured her.

"But it was kind of Gili to stay in the tent with the guards so Sasha and I could remain in his house."

"It was the least we could do when you've canceled our debt for the vineyard," Gili said.

Naama turned and went into the house to stir the stew while everyone else celebrated outside. When Ariel followed her into the kitchen, he heard her sniffling.

"What's wrong?"

Naama shuddered. "I'm sorry. I know you worked hard on the wall and it's a wonderful accomplishment, but...I have an overwhelming feeling Yael needs us *now*. Not later, after the celebration."

Ariel considered her words. "I think you're right. At any rate, she's been in Rabbah long enough. David and I will go with Judith as soon as she's ready."

"I hope you arrive in time."

"We'll pray for her tonight before our meal." Ariel squeezed her arm.

Naama nodded and resumed seasoning the stew.

⌘⌘

The next morning Judith, her servants, Ariel, and David left as the sun rose. Judith shared Naama's feelings of urgency. *Would the girl be fit to wed by the time her brother and his household finished with her?*

Tobiah treated his servants callously, as did most of the men in Rabbah and Persia. More than one maid had disappeared from Ctesias' household after a dalliance with the master or one of the older boys.

Judith shuddered. It had never bothered her before. She hadn't seen it happen in Gibeon. The Gibeonites were too poor to have servants, but she couldn't imagine it was common practice in Yehud, even in Jerusalem, where some families engaged servants.

Before they reached the main road, a messenger appeared ahead of them. "Master Ctesias and the caravan

174

left Jerusalem this morning. He said to go east toward Rabbah rather than south toward Jerusalem."

David pumped his fist in the air.

Judith rejoiced inwardly. It should take two days to arrive in Rabbah. When they were close enough, she could take a few men and ride ahead to Tobiah's.

41

We have to go back, Yael," Johanan explained. "The chief goatherd has never seen snow so early in the season. This will melt, but it's going to be a long, hard winter. We're going to move all the goats closer to town, maybe put some in father's courtyard."

"Your mother won't like animals fouling her courtyard."

"No," Johanan grinned, "but my siblings will."

Yael smiled a little and twisted her robe with thin fingers. "I'm afraid to return."

"I know, but I was planning to buy my own home. I'll speed up the process. You and Eden can look at property too."

"She resents me. She's going to be harder to deal with than usual."

"I know, but I love you, so you'll get a say in the house."

"Johanan..."

"You haven't accepted me yet, but we should let everyone think I've claimed you. You'll be safer."

"I don't want to lie."

"We don't have to say anything. The household will assume, and their assumptions should keep you safe. It will give you time to hear back from father's sister. We'll relocate to my new home as quickly as possible.

"Eden wasn't pleased about living with the rest of the family, so she and mother may have already started looking for a place."

⌘⌘

A caravan guard called to the horse boys to open the courtyard gate. Hearing the commotion, household members began gathering.

Judith recognized Tobiah's wife Abigail and his second wife but no one else. Four children, several servants, and a teenaged girl milled around the courtyard.

"Judith, you look as lovely as always," Abigail greeted her. "What brings you here?" She dispatched a servant to find Tobiah. "Come inside for a drink and some fruit."

David and Ariel followed Judith into the hallway.

"Who's this?" Tobiah demanded.

"Shalom, brother." Judith used her silkiest, yet most authoritative voice.

"Judith? I'd know that voice anywhere," Tobiah said. "Welcome, sister. What a surprise!"

"I'm sure it is. We have business to discuss with these good men."

Tobiah's gaze swung to Ariel and David, and his face hardened. "They've come with the payment for your dowry?"

"They've ridden a long way," Abigail interrupted. "Let's talk over some refreshment."

Tobiah turned and led the group into a room with a long low table and plush rugs scattered on the floor. Servants brought water and wine.

"Your oldest nephew is out with the goats," Tobiah told Judith. "This is his wife, Eden."

Judith nodded to the attractive teenager over her cup of wine. Setting it down, she said to Tobiah, "About my vineyard... Could you and I discuss the matter privately?"

Tobiah rose and led his sister to an anteroom out of earshot of the dining area.

"Brother, I appreciate your diligence in looking out for my affairs," Judith flattered, "but as you know I married Ctesias the Persian. His business thrives. The jewelry I'm wearing to travel is worth more than the measly price of my dowry."

"But to send you away in disgrace! Their family owes us," Tobiah insisted.

"The gods smiled on me. You've seen Ariel's wife?"

"Not an attractive thing about her."

"She's worn down by hard work in the vineyard. It could have been my fate, but I got away from scrabbling in that piece of dirt. Not to mention it barely supports them. They can't even afford to age the wine properly. I'm lucky I left."

"You could never look like that woman. You look as magnificent as always, Judith."

"Thank you," Judith preened to play along. "But if I'd stayed there, my hands would be red and chapped, my face would be rough and lined, my body bent.

"I'm glad to be rid of that rocky vineyard. Let them break their backs and hearts over it. You didn't know, but Benjamin and I spoke of the debt. He settled with me."

"For the full price?" Tobiah tried to guess the meaning of her turn of phrase.

178

"Every last clod of dirt has been paid for," Judith said coolly. "Now, I've brought you presents. I know your wife misses Judean honey, so I've plenty, but also some bangles for your girls and cinnamon and other spices for you."

⌘⌘

In the dining chamber, Abigail broke the tense silence. "How are things in Gibeon?"

"The harvest was fair," Ariel answered. "Last I knew, your father was well. I saw him in Jerusalem a little more than a moon ago. He now has a stout gate to tend, rather than an honorary title."

"I'm sure that makes him happy. He tried to regulate the comings and goings, but anyone could enter at night. If I send a message to father, could you take it to him next time you go to Jerusalem?"

"I can take it when we attend the feast later this month," Ariel said.

Eden leaned in close to David as she refilled his cup of spiced wine. "It's a shame you didn't arrive last week."

"We got here as fast as we could, certainly a lot faster than waiting for a messenger to and from Susa."

"Yes, but it's too late for both our marriages."

"What do you mean?"

"Johanan claimed Yael as his concubine and took her out to the herds to keep her away from Tobiah."

"What?" David yelled.

Abigail and Ariel froze.

"Is this true?" Ariel asked Abigail.

"My husband was enraged with your daughter. Johanan protected her."

The men sat in stunned silence until David ripped his cloak in one fierce movement. "I can't see her, Ariel. Not with *him*."

"We're expecting them any time," Abigail said quietly. "They're bringing the herds in from pasture due to the early cold. We won't have room for you here once they return because Judith and Ctesias will settle in the guest quarters. I'll send a servant to Dael, brother of Benjamin, to inquire about accommodations there, if you'd like."

"We would appreciate that," Ariel said, tugging David to his feet. "I think we'll gather our borrowed horses and ride toward the market while we wait for Judith and Tobiah to finish.

"Could you have your servant meet us there? If Dael can't accommodate us, we'll stay at the caravansary with Ctesias' caravan. I'm sure we could find space to lay our mats."

"As the sun sets, my servant will look for you in the spice sellers' area." Abigail gestured to one of the male servants and turned to usher the men into the courtyard, calling two stable boys to fetch their guests' horses.

"I'm sorry. Truly I am. I'll look out for her. Johanan will continue to, also. She's a very special girl." Abigail stopped at the hurt on the men's two faces. "I'm so sorry.

"I should get back to my husband and his sister, so you don't have to face them right now. I'll make sure Yael sends a letter to her mother."

Ariel bundled David onto the horse lent by Benjamin and hurried out the gates before David could react.

180

42

The moon lit the way for Johanan and Yael to herd a dozen goats into the courtyard. Yael glanced at the wall where Tobiah had cornered her and shuddered.

"Slip into the house and sleep in the children's room, as you usually do," Johanan instructed. As a few servants exited the house to tend the animals, Yael hurried to do his bidding, praying to avoid Tobiah.

Eden poked her head out the door of Johanan's sleeping room, but said nothing.

Yael crept carefully around the little ones, hoping her mat was still in the corner. Noa stirred and mumbled, but none of them wakened. Finding the mat, Yael curled up, pulled a rug over herself, and prayed for protection from her enemies.

Unfortunately, the only enemies I have live in this house. Adonai, please let me go home, and give Johanan and Eden a new place, one where I could hide for a while, if need be. Comforted by her prayers, she fell into a deep sleep.

Consciousness returned with a delicious sense of warmth. The last few days in tents had been colder than she wanted to admit. When her brain registered the weight of a warm body against her back, her eyes popped open. For a minute, Yael thought... But it was only Noa snuggled up to her.

Yael's eyes surveyed the room, skidding to a stop at the door where Eden stood, glaring malevolently.

At least it's not Tobiah, and Johanan's not the one keeping my back warm. Yael eased away from the sleeping Noa, pulled on her sandals, and pointed toward the hall.

"Before you say *anything*, nothing's happened between me and your husband. I'd like to keep it that way." Yael spoke softly and glanced nervously down the hall for eavesdroppers. "I just want to go home and marry David."

Eden's ugly expression changed to...something Yael couldn't identify. "I'd like that too." Eden seemed nervous. "I'll help if I can. Unfortunately, I already... Listen, Johanan's aunt who owned the vineyard and your father and betrothed arrived yesterday."

A shock passed through Yael. Her cares fell away, and she beamed.

"Only Judith stayed for the night. I think the others ended up with the rug merchant."

"Dael?" Yael asked.

"Is he the brother of Benjamin?"

"Yes. Benjamin used to be married to Judith."

Eden looked a little confused. "I'll have to get Abigail to explain later. Right now you need to hurry over there. The sun's already up. I hope they're still there."

"Why wouldn't they still be at Dael's?"

"I'll have to explain it to you later. Hurry. I'll arrange your hair."

182

"Let me sneak back in to get my headdress."

"No time. You can wear my headdress," Eden said, starting to finger comb Yael's sleep-tangled hair. Yael started on the other side.

"Good enough to be covered," Eden announced a few moments later. They'd walked to Johanan's chamber while smoothing out the knots. Relieved he wasn't there, Yael arranged Eden's headscarf over her own dark hair.

"Take my horse, so Tobiah doesn't accuse you of horse theft," Eden said. "Go quickly now."

Yael hurried out of the house and waited impatiently while a boy brought the gray mare. She used a rock to mount and exited the courtyard as swiftly as possible before realizing she didn't know where Dael lived. She only knew the location of his shop.

She urged the mare into a canter and headed for the marketplace. The guard would know where to send her.

As she navigated the city streets, Yael chewed some figs Cook had shoved into her hand. The colder weather squelched the smell of refuse, so Yael counted it as a blessing to offset her cold fingers.

The proximity of her family made her feel like singing. Due to the early hour and public setting, she settled for humming. *"I will lift up my eyes to the hills; from where shall my help come? My help comes from the Lord, the maker of heaven and earth."*

An hour's wait in the cold dampened her enthusiasm, but the guard finally appeared and opened the shop for Dael, who arrived shortly after and greeted her fondly. "I hear you'll be staying with us in Rabbah?" he asked.

"No. Judith is here and can confirm my family's vineyard is paid for," Yael replied. "Has she not spoken with her brother yet? We returned late last night with the goats, and I didn't see anyone this morning other than

183

Eden. She thought my father and David were staying with you."

Dael looked somber. "They only stayed for a short period of refreshment. They returned to Yehud yesterday with the king's mail courier."

"But why didn't they wait for me?" Yael cried. "I'm free to go home. More than anything, I want to go home."

Dael paused and then suggested, "Let's go back to Tobiah's and sort out what's going on."

"Tobiah is the last person I want to see. He was ready to kill me last time I saw him."

"I heard, and I also heard Johanan claimed you as his concubine."

"Yes, to keep me safe, but we didn't..." The blood drained from Yael's face. "Abba and David think I'm a concubine?"

"Yes, but if you're not..."

"I most definitely am not. Johanan will swear to it as well. I will be able to offer proof on my wedding night, but..."

"Let's deal with one problem at a time. Come back to Tobiah's with me. He won't try to harm you while I'm there. We'll take one of my guards and another merchant or two as witnesses."

Dael boosted her back onto the mare and gave a servant instructions for running the shop. As he guided the mare through the morning marketplace, Dael asked one of the spice merchants to accompany them.

How will I get home? Will David still want me? Will he trust me? I can't give him any proof until our wedding night.

⌘⌘

"Yael, daughter of Ariel, you've had quite the time of it these past six moons, haven't you?" Judith asked in a low voice as the men greeted each other in Tobiah's front hall.

At Yael's look of surprise, Judith continued, "I'd know you anywhere, dear. You look just like your mother when I met her." She smiled at the memory. "Slimmer though. She was very pregnant."

Before Yael knew what had happened, Cook whisked her into the warm kitchen and handed her a cup of hot tea while Judith met with the men.

Eden crept in and cowered before her. "I'm sorry, Yael. I'm the one who told David you'd become a concubine."

"You didn't know any better, Eden."

"I know better than to spring the news on him heartlessly."

"I can't fault you for wanting your husband to yourself. Treat him well, and he may not take another wife."

"I meant to. It's just I've been so homesick. I didn't realize he might marry again until we came here and I saw all the men who keep multiple wives. It's not done in Yehud, though I know it was in the past."

"Gives you sympathy for Rachel and Leah, doesn't it?" Yael asked wryly. "Anyway, all I want is to go home."

"I don't know how to get you home, but I know Someone who does." Eden put her hand on Yael's shoulder and prayed. "*El Roi,* God who sees us and our predicament, please take Yael back to her family. Heal the relationship with her betrothed, and make her as fruitful as our mother Leah."

Yael was staring at her with her mouth gaping when Eden finished. "I didn't know you could pray so beautifully."

Eden smiled shyly. "I did learn *something* as a priest's daughter, but I've been focused on pitying myself and haven't been praying much lately. Sometimes I think it's easier to pray for someone else," she paused. "My abba taught me to make amends with those I've wronged before I pray for myself. Will you forgive me for what I've done?"

Although doubtful Eden owed an apology for being jealous of her husband's attentions, Yael assured her, "Absolutely. And I'd appreciate it if you'd help me keep out of Tobiah's way."

"I promise I'll do what I can."

⌘⌘

"Our caravan departs tomorrow," Judith told Yael later in the afternoon. "Dael said you could stay with his family until a caravan heading to Yehud passes through Rabbah. I'm sorry I can't get you home sooner."

"You've done so much for me already. Thank you. Adonai arranged for you to be in Yehud when we needed you."

If only I were there when Tobiah first stormed into the vineyard and disrupted your life, but your faith is touching. "Since Benjamin and I had already agreed the vineyard was paid, Abigail will pay you for your months of service. Just don't mention it to Tobiah."

"I'm trying to avoid Tobiah," Yael said. "I won't be talking with him."

186

"Johanan will take you to Dael's tonight, but I wanted to make sure I said good-bye." Judith embraced her.

"Shalom, and thank you, Judith."

"Here's Johanan now. May your Lord bless you and keep you, Yael."

"Aunt Judith, forgive me for the interruption, but Father's gone out on business. If Yael packs quickly, we can leave before he returns," Johanan said. "I'll be in the courtyard, readying our mounts, Yael. I'll see you at dinner, Aunt Judith."

Johanan stopped the horses on the sand-swept street leading to Dael's impressive home. "I'm sorry to see you go, Yael. Are you sure I can't convince you to stay?"

"Yes, my place is with David in Yehud."

"I was afraid you'd say that. This is good-bye for us then. I won't visit before you leave."

"Thank you for looking out for me. I wouldn't be able to return if it weren't for your protection." The two continued to the gate of Dael's stone home.

"Johanan, your wife craves your attention. She's been whiny because she was homesick. I think a home of her own will make her more content."

"Wise words, my friend. I'll be sure to heed them." Johanan handed her bag to the servant monitoring Dael's door. "Shalom, Yael."

"Peace be on you and your house."

43

Jarah rejoiced her boys had not inherited her singing voice. "'I was glad when they said to me...'" She stopped singing and listened to the boys enthusiastically finish, "'let us go to the house of the Lord!'"

She smiled and continued with them. "'Pray for the peace of Jerusalem: They shall prosper that love thee. Peace be within thy walls....'"

Jarah fell silent, remembering the first time she and Oren entered Jerusalem singing these psalms. There were no walls, and she had longed to rebuild, and for sons to share the labor.

"God, you are so good," she whispered, admiring her four sturdy sons.

"Em, how does the next one start?" Doran demanded.

"'To You I lift up my eyes, O You who are enthroned in the heavens,'" Judith began. Ariel and Menachem's families joined the joyful strains.

"Why are we singing on this trip?" Gedalya asked.

"We're going to celebrate the Feast of Tabernacles. Singing and worshipping God prepare our hearts," Oren said.

"Don't you remember coming last year?" nine-year-old Hoshea asked his younger brother.

"Not really," Gedalya admitted.

"You were only three, Son. This year will be different anyway. When Ezra read the words of the law this month, our leaders realized this should be a week-long celebration. We're going to build huts and camp out. "

"Are we going to have to stand up all day and listen to priests read?" Doran asked in alarm, remembering the lengthy Scripture reading to celebrate the completion of the wall.

"Not *all* day," Jabin corrected. "I liked the part where Levite Bani answered our questions."

"And the dinner we ate with Priest Ezra's family was the *best*!" Hoshea added. "I liked having my questions answered too," he added hastily, catching his mother's reproving look.

Oren laughed. "I enjoyed the feast too. We'll listen to God's Word *and* share special meals with our friends this week. Not tonight though. Tonight we'll take the olive and myrtle branches we brought from Gibeon and fashion a booth."

"Where are we going to build it?" Gedalya asked.

"In the courtyard of our home," Oren said. "Ariel's family will build one next to ours."

"What about Eliezer's family?" Jabin asked of his best friend.

"Our courtyard's not big enough for any more booths, but you can still see him," Jarah promised. "Find out where they plan to build theirs."

Jabin trotted over to Eliezer who was leading a donkey with his youngest brother astride. After a brief exchange, he bounced back to his mother. "They'll try to set up in the temple courtyard."

"Excellent. We'll meet at temple every day." Jarah made a mental note to invite Tova's family to sup with them since her pregnancy slowed her down. It would be a challenging week for her friend, who needed extra rest. Perhaps Adonai would bless her with a daughter this time.

Adonai, while I'm thinking of it, I also ask for a daughter.

Jarah's gaze turned to Naama, who plodded along stoically, pulling Nasha by the hand. After riding their ancient donkey most of the way, the five-year-old had given her seat to her seven-year-old brother Saul.

Little Ebin rode on his Uncle Gili's back while Ariel caught his breath after carrying him most of the way.

Naama was taking the news of Yael's concubine status hard. The empty look in her eyes scared Jarah.

The older children passed myrtle and palm branches to their fathers and Uncle Gili, who overlapped them to construct three huts.

When the men departed for the evening sacrifice, Jarah and Naama began to prepare a meal, while Ebin slept on a goatskin.

The women added water to barley flour and formed circles of unleavened dough while stirring lentils over two fires started by Jabin and Hoshea.

"How are things with you?" Jarah finally asked in the silence.

"Fine," Naama answered without thinking. "The journey passed quickly and without problems."

190

Jarah took the wooden stick from her friend's hand and captured both hands in hers. "This is me, your friend. I can tell you're *not* fine."

Naama's lips quivered. "I've lost both my firstborn son *and* daughter, Jarah."

Jarah realized the present sorrow was opening Naama's old wounds. "I miss her too, but she lives."

"I'll never see her again." Naama's tears fell.

Jarah patted her back. "Johanan seems like a good man."

"His father is a wicked heathen."

"But he has a good mother, and we know Johanan is a protector," Jarah comforted.

Naama sighed. "I miss my em more than anything else I left in Susa. Our life in the vineyard is hard, but I hoped to keep my children near.

"Yael has loved David for years. She has never looked at any other man. For her to be bound to *Johanan*," Naama almost spat his name, "must be infinitely painful. She has such a loyal heart."

"Adonai may place her on a new path. He hasn't forgotten her. Remember His words—'Can a woman forget her nursing child and have no compassion on the son of her womb? Even these may forget, but I will not forget you.'

"You would never forget Yael. And Adonai will never forget Yael....or you."

"Why does it feel like He has?" Naama wailed.

"Sometimes how we feel doesn't match what's true."

Jarah's heart remained heavy for Naama as they stood to hear God's words the next morning.

After sacrificing a lamb, High Priest Eliashib read from the law of Moses with a strong voice belying his age. His eldest son Joiada read the Creation of the world. The other two sons read of Noah and father Abraham.

The Levites sang several psalms including "For a day in your courts is better than a thousand outside." Jarah sang along softly. *Will Yael get to worship here again?*

Naama and Nasha left the assembly when Ebin became fretful. Naama also took Gedalya so Jarah could stay with the older children.

After her mother departed, Raisa pressed close to Jarah's side. Guessing she missed her sister, Jarah put an arm around the ten-year-old's shoulders.

When the sun was high, Ezra dismissed the crowds.

After roasted grain and figs washed down with Ariel and Gili's wine, the men took the boys back to the temple. Oren wanted to check on supplies of wood and water. Jabin itched to find Eliezer and explore Jerusalem. The younger boys could play together and help their fathers as needed.

"I can't believe Gedalya is old enough to be included in almost everything his father does," Jarah lamented to Naama. "I miss having a little one." She held out her arms for a fussy Ebin and rocked him until his eyes closed.

"It's hard to let go of our children....even harder to think they've been taken," Naama said softly, gazing at her son's peaceful face.

"We often don't get a choice," Jarah agreed, carefully settling Ebin on his goatskin bed.

"Before I left with our little ones, I heard the writings about Father Abraham and Isaac. He was prepared to give up his son as a sacrifice. To kill the son of promise in obedience to Adonai."

Naama's voice fell to a whisper. "I think I need to do the same, with my Yael. Not kill her, like Judith did to Hen, but give her up to whatever purpose the Almighty has."

"Very wise," Jarah said.

"But not easy."

"No, but Adonai will help you."

"How do I start?"

Judith thought for a long moment. "How about a prayer for strength?"

Naama nodded. "Will you pray with me?" Both women lifted their hands to the heavens.

"Father God," Naama began. "You know my heart is broken, and you know how my Yael is. You gave her to me thirteen years ago. Please watch over her.

"You said you're present in our trouble. Seems like we've had lots of trouble in this land, but I thank you for the vineyard. It makes my husband and Gili happy, gives them purpose. Thank you for letting us keep it. But God, it was at the price of my daughter. My innocent daughter who can't even share in its fruits any more."

Naama's voice broke. "I don't understand, but I give her to you. If you could, I'd like to hear of her soon, to know she's well."

"I agree with Naama's words, *El Roi*. You see us here, two mothers grieving Yael's fate. Let her husband treat her with kindness and understanding. Protect her from harm, and bring peace to her mother's heart."

"Thank you." Naama wiped away her tears with the back of her hand.

She turned the lamb, roasting on a spit over the fire. "I hope this will feed all of us. It's hard to keep the children's bellies full."

"It should be enough with the leavened bread I started last night," Jarah said.

"Abraham nearly sacrificing his son is a strange story, don't you think? For a God who's against human sacrifice."

"I think it was more about what Abraham was willing to do in obedience to God. And he came out of Ur, where human sacrifice was practiced. God hadn't given Moses the teachings against human sacrifice yet."

⌘⌘

Naama relaxed and began enjoying the time in Jerusalem after her decision. Both Naama and Jarah's families ate a meal with Hadassah and Benjamin and their two little girls. The boys vied for the attention of Rachel and Hallel with their antics and games.

Jarah started considering marriages among the families and added Tova's boys to her schemes. She also kept an eye on Gili to see if he favored any of the women at the feast. At his age, he might even marry a widow with children.

Nehemiah invited all of them to a huge feast. Jarah calculated a hundred people dined on oxen and mutton. She brought a length of cloth as a gift, and Ariel presented a jar of wine. Naama whispered to her, "I've never eaten such a feast!"

Jarah compared the extravagant, yet uncomfortable meals at her uncle Ezekiel's home in Susa to the friendly, festive atmosphere at the Tirshatha's. *Thank you for bringing me to this place, Adonai, and giving me this amazing family.*

194

"Stop shoveling food into your mouth, Doran. There's plenty. Gedalya, chew with your mouth closed." *About that daughter, Lord...*

A week sped by with daily readings and offerings at the temple. Jarah weaved white linen during the afternoons. She watched over Ebin along with Gedalya while they napped so Naama could explore the city and visit with Hadassah.

It rained two days in a row. Jarah would be glad to get home to Gibeon and sleep under a solid roof again.

⌘⌘

On the last day of the feast, all men, women, and children gathered at the temple to bring their offerings. Naama tried to corral the children as they followed Ariel and Gili to make a drink offering with their best, aged wine.

As the rich red liquid flowed onto the altar, she prayed silently. *Everything we have is yours, Adonai, our best wine, the vines, our land, and our children. You've taken Otanes and Yael, but I've tried to hold onto them anyway. Now I choose to give them to you, like Abraham gave Isaac.*

Remind me Yael is yours when I try to take her back through worry. Thank you for your gifts—Ariel and all these little ones you've given me.

As they turned to leave, Naama looked away from her family and surreptitiously wiped her tears with her headdress. Raisa squeezed her arm. "I miss Yael too."

"God is watching over her. I'm sure of it," Naama assured the older child while taking Nasha's small hand in her own. "And He's watching over us too."

They returned to their booths for one last evening, lingering around the cook fire in the cooling air. Tomorrow

195

they would rise early and return to Gibeon and their labor in the vineyards.

44

Naama's family limped up the road to their vineyard. Raisa and Saul dragged their feet as each toted a small bundle. Ebin's arms wrapped around his father's broad shoulders.

Gili led the donkey, which had gone lame halfway through the daylong trip. This donkey had traveled with them from Susa. It wouldn't live much longer. Their younger animal, left home with her foal, nickered as she caught the scent of her stablemate.

Naama's muddy toes chafed in her sandals. They needed to be replaced. Ariel could work on making new ones this rainy season, along with pairs for Raisa and Ebin.

Naama looked forward to long evenings around the fire with her family busy at various tasks while she finished the rug delayed by her burnt hands. She flexed her fingers. The scar tissue reduced their suppleness, but Jarah's ministrations had restored much of their function. *Praise Adonai!*

Gili split off to care for the donkey just before their home came into view. Strange, a ribbon of smoke rose from the outside hearth.

Naama's heart thumped in alarm. No one should be here to offer a homecoming. More trouble?

Raisa dropped her goatskin bag full of their leavened bread and ran toward the house. Releasing Nasha's hand, Naama tiredly regathered it, resigned to giving her daughter a good scolding.

Saul was shouting, and Nasha dashed off. What had gotten into them?

She focused on the figure rising from a pot at the fire, and froze. "Yael?"

Her eldest was gathering her siblings for hugs and then heading toward her. Dropping all her gear, Naama stepped into her daughter's embrace, stroking her hair. "What happened? You're not a concubine?"

"No, Em. I'm fine, ready to marry David if he'll still have me. Come, sit. You look worn out."

Ariel clasped Yael to his chest until a muffled "I can't breathe, Abba" caused him to release her. "Saul, take a fresh donkey and go find David. Tell him his bride has safely returned to him."

"But how did you get here?" Naama asked.

"I came with Benjamin's brother Dael. His caravan went on to Jerusalem, but he brought me safely home, said he'd easily catch up with a slow-moving caravan. You probably passed them."

Naama remembered moving aside for a caravan. She touched her daughter's face. "Has anyone hurt you? I can't believe you're here."

"No, Adonai protected me. I'll tell you what happened while we eat. I made flat bread and vegetable stew."

"I didn't expect a hot meal tonight."

Raisa brought water. Gili retrieved a jar from the cistern where they aged wine. "Tonight we celebrate!"

198

They settled around the fire to eat. A piece of bread in hand, Nasha cuddled up to her sister. Raisa sat on Yael's other side, close enough to touch her. With Ebin in her lap, Naama sat across from her.

Thank you for protecting her, God. Thank you for bringing her back. Let David take her as his wife.

Raisa fired questions at her sister. Ariel added more, but Naama just listened, drinking in the sight of her. Yael's cheeks were flushed, her manner happy and carefree.

In less time than Naama would have thought possible, David came barreling into the yard with Saul and the donkey in hot pursuit. "Yael, I'm so glad you're back. We heard..." he faltered, inhaling deeply to catch his breath.

Yael bit her lip and twisted her bread into pieces in her lap. "I didn't become anyone's concubine. Johanan offered, in order to protect me from Tobiah. He took me out to the goats' pastures, but nothing happened between us. Of course I can't prove it until..."

"Don't say another word. When can we have the ceremony?" David asked.

Gili whooped, and the children joined in.

Yael blushed. "In two weeks?"

"Done," Ariel said quickly.

How will we prepare enough food for the wedding feast? Jarah's in Jerusalem while Oren replenishes stores at the temple, and Tova's pregnant.

"And look, Abigail paid me three silver coins for my service. Judith arranged it with her. She said since the vineyard had been paid for all along, I deserved wages." Yael beamed with pride at bringing earnings into her marriage.

David looked a bit stricken, but Ariel rescued him, saying, "Come see all the hard work David's put into your section of vineyard. He's tripled the number of plantings."

199

Naama swiftly stored their gear and washed out the cooking pot while everyone else but Gili and Ebin trooped off to view the vineyard. Gili deposited his nephew on a sleeping mat, telling the story of David and Goliath until the travel-exhausted toddler's eyes closed.

"Adonai is good," he said, passing Naama on his way to his cozy home.

"His mercy endures forever," Naama agreed.

Epilogue

5 years later

Naama cuddled the bundle in her lap as she minded the stew bubbling on the outdoor fire. She ran a finger down her granddaughter's cheek and was rewarded with a toothless smile. The baby's twin brother fussed in Yael's arms as Nasha kneaded bread.

Yael's babies had required all Naama's skill to birth and coax to health. Now they thrived, without any sign of the tiny, frail creatures they had been at birth. They joined their big brother in wreaking havoc on any of Naama's plans to slow down now that she was a softa.

Warmth seeped into Naama from the coals, pushing back the cool damp of a day long past harvest. The harvest this year had been bountiful, *praise Adonai*. Enough to support Naama's family as well as Yael's growing brood.

In the years since Yael's return to the vineyard, the family experienced both drought and abundance. But best of all, they were together. Raisa had married Jarah's firstborn son Jabin and lived nearby in Gibeon.

Naama started to sing, "'I will lift up my eyes to the hills; from where shall my help come?'"

Yael and Nasha joined the anthem. "'My help comes from the Lord, the maker of heaven and earth.'"

Acknowledgments

Thanks to:

Nadine Lahan for content editing

Jeff Spires for formatting

Sharon Spires for critiquing and editing

Marc Velez for formatting

Christian Writers' Group of San Antonio members: Al Bates, Terri Beardman, Nancy Christy, Sandy Cleary, Monica Clegg, Cathey Edgington, April Gardner, Jim Hopper, Van Mabrito. Your critiques made this a better book.

28088138R00128

Made in the USA
Middletown, DE
19 December 2018